W9-BKP-511

CARRYING HER MILLIONAIRE'S BABY

CARRYING HER MILLIONAIRE'S BABY

SOPHIE PEMBROKE

MILLS & BOON

First published in Great Britain 2019
by Mills & Boon, an imprint of HarperCollins*Publishers*
1 London Bridge Street, London, SE1 9GF

Large Print edition 2019

© 2019 Sophie Pembroke

ISBN: 978-0-263-08278-4

MIX
Paper from
responsible sources
FSC® C007454

This book is produced from independently certified
FSC™ paper to ensure responsible forest management. For
more information visit www.harpercollins.co.uk/green.

Printed and bound in Great Britain
by CPI Group (UK) Ltd, Croydon, CR0 4YY

For Hayley,
with love and takeaway curry x

CHAPTER ONE

ZOEY HEPBURN SHOVED the hotel window a little further open, hoisted her bare foot up onto the sill and cursed as her hem got caught on the latch—again. She was beginning to regret the strapless hot pink dress she'd chosen for her rehearsal dinner. However pretty the lacy skirt was, it was not getaway-friendly.

Of course, when she bought it, she hadn't been planning on escaping through a back window the night before her wedding. But then, she never did.

'People are looking for you, you know.' The calm, almost lazy voice behind her made Zoey jump just enough to whack her head on the window frame. *Ow.* 'Also, you made me promise I wouldn't let you do this again this time.'

'Again feels a little harsh. I've never actually climbed out of a window before.' Maybe her shoulders would fit through the small gap better if she twisted them more to the left.

Zoey tried it. They wouldn't.

Ash sighed. His usual, *What did I do in a past life to get lumbered with you as my friend?* sigh. Zoey was alarmingly familiar with it.

'They want to do the speeches,' he said. As if the idea of hearing David's father waffle on about how important his family was—to him and to the world at large—might tempt her back into the hotel restaurant. Everyone in there knew what trouble his company was in anyway, whatever tall tales he told about famous people he'd met once and who would never remember his name.

David didn't do that, she reminded herself. David was reasonably modest. Well, compared to his father anyway, which wasn't a *very* high bar, she had to admit.

Still, it meant she probably couldn't use 'pompous name-dropper' as a reason for not marrying him.

'Since when did speeches become a must for rehearsal dinners, anyway?' she asked, eyeing the window again. 'Can't they save them for tomorrow? You know, the *actual* wedding.'

'Seems to me they're being sensible getting them in early,' Ash said, and she just *knew* he was raising an eyebrow at her, the way he always used to when she and Grace came home from the pub tipsy and tried to deny that last bottle of wine they'd shared. 'Tomorrow is not looking like a sure thing right now.'

Outside, a warm breeze fluttered past like butterfly wings. She was in paradise—a luxurious island in the middle of the Indian ocean, a boutique hotel filled with her and David's friends and family, private villas on stilts stretching out into the azure sea from a wooden boardwalk for all her guests.

It was just unfortunate that, from the minute she'd arrived three days ago for the last-minute wedding preparations, she'd felt as if she'd been trapped in purgatory.

But she wasn't going to escape hell through

this window—even if she *had* followed any of those 'Lose Ten Pounds for your Wedding Day' diets her mother had kept leaving strategically around the house. Which she hadn't.

Resigned, Zoey pulled her head back through the open window, turned to face her best friend's husband and sat down on the windowsill. 'I can't go back in there, Ash.'

Ash took a seat on the table she'd climbed up on to reach the window. 'Because rehearsal dinners are a terrible tradition that should be banned, or because you don't want to marry David tomorrow?'

'Both,' Zoey replied promptly. 'And I should know. I've had three rehearsal dinners, including this one.'

'And not a wedding between them,' Ash said mournfully. 'Not to mention the two other broken engagements.'

Zoey winced. 'Three, actually. One of them was before Grace and I met you.'

'The musician, right?' Ash tilted his head to the side as he looked at her. 'Grace told me about him. I think calling that one off was legit.'

'As opposed to the others?' She gave him a sideways look. 'Do you honestly think I should have married Harry, or Julian, or Fred?'

'I suppose not.' Leaning back, Ash rested his elbows on the table and looked up at her. His bright blue eyes were too knowing, and Zoey had to work to resist the urge to brush his sooty hair away from them. He really was absurdly good-looking. The thought registered, as it always did—an acknowledgement of a fact, like saying the ocean was blue.

She'd never let herself dwell on it beyond that. That way lay madness and misery.

'It's just a shame you never figured out that they weren't the right guy for you until the morning of the wedding,' Ash went on, and she focused on his words rather than his looks again. 'As much as *I* love a last-minute runaway bride drama, I think some other people might be thinking it's gone a little far now.'

He could have a point, Zoey allowed. In

fact, she had a nagging suspicion that David might have had an ulterior motive for insisting the wedding took place on an island in the middle of nowhere.

She frowned. Ash would know. 'When David spoke to you about booking the wedding, did he say why he wanted to have it here?' She hadn't wanted to ask before. But if not now, when?

Ash, as heir to the Carmichael Luxury Travel business, had organised the use of the island hotel as his wedding present to them. She was pretty sure his company actually owned the island, as well as the hotel, when it came down to it. Zoey wondered if she'd have to pay him back for that if the wedding didn't go ahead. She hoped not. Her job as an art gallery assistant in London was her dream, but the benefits weren't all entirely financial.

'He might have mentioned the advantages of having control over which boats and sea planes arrived at—and more pertinently left—the island,' Ash said diplomatically.

'You mean he was trying to make sure I couldn't run away.' Zoey frowned. Was *He manipulated my wedding venue choice* a good enough excuse not to marry him? And why did she need an excuse at all beyond *I don't want to*?

Because your mother is going to pitch a fit. Not to mention all the other people you're letting down.

Not Ash, though. Even if he had gone along with David's possibly nefarious scheme.

'Why didn't you tell me that sooner?' she asked, trying to feel outraged and failing. 'I mean, you'd let me marry a man who didn't give me an out on my wedding day? What kind of a friend are you?'

Ash rolled his eyes. 'Yes, obviously this is my fault. Zoey, you know that if you told me you wanted out then I would get you out—planes, boats and automobiles be damned. But, if you recall, you also told me—quite definitely—when we had dinner last month that David was *absolutely* the one, and that I wasn't to let you get cold feet this time, because you'd regret it for the rest of your life.'

Had she really said that? It was hard to imagine somehow, here and now. Impossible to summon up that certainty again—and not because of the island, or his father's pompous speeches. But because now it came down to it she simply could not picture spending the rest of her life with David.

But she *had* been able to once. She must have done, to say yes to his proposal. She'd loved him—or believed she did—and had been planning their life together right up until the moment they had arrived in paradise to get married.

People might laugh at her history of running out on weddings—and, yes, there had been a few family members who'd refused to even come to this one, just in case—but when she said yes to a guy on one knee with a sparkly ring, she always, *always* meant it.

It was just getting from 'yes' to 'I do' that seemed to cause her problems.

Her whole life with just one person—that

was a big ask. And Zoey had seen first-hand what a disaster it could be if she picked the wrong one. Her own parents were a shining example of how not to do marriage.

And then there was Ash.

Ash, her only friend, who had been her best friend's husband. Ash, who'd had the perfect marriage—until it had been ripped away from him and had left him broken.

Zoey bit her lip, contemplating the question she wanted to ask but didn't know if she dared.

'What?' Ash sat up straighter, watching her. 'Whatever it is, just ask, Zoey. You know I'll help if I can.'

He always had. Ash was one of only two people she'd known beyond doubt that she'd always be able to rely on, ever since she and Grace had met him in the student union over a decade earlier. But she didn't want to hurt him by bringing up painful memories.

On the other hand, she needed to know the answer, if she were to make a real decision about what to do next—not just bash her way through a window and hope for the best.

'When you and Grace...on your wedding day. Weren't you nervous?'

Unbidden, memories of that perfect English summer day came back to her. Grace, her best friend since junior school, ethereally beautiful in her delicate lace dress. Zoey's rose-pink bridesmaid's dress, a perfect match for the tea roses in Grace's bouquet. The tiny stone chapel in their home village. The afternoon tea reception on the village green, with mismatched china and bunting strung all around.

And, through it all, Ash and Grace smiling at each other as if their hearts were on show. So in love, so certain that the future would be perfect, as long as they were together.

It hurt now to think of how happy they'd all been, never imagining that it could all be torn away from them in a heartbeat.

'Nervous?' Ash shook his head. 'I was terrified.'

He hadn't looked it. He'd seemed like a man whose every dream had come true.

If Ash had been nervous, maybe it was okay that she was too?

Or maybe it depended on why. Because Ash had gone through with it. He'd said 'I do' and promised his whole life to another person.

And six diamond rings later, that was something Zoey still hadn't managed.

Ash took in the look of confusion on Zoey's face and wondered how he could make her understand, when the depth and strength of his love for Grace had always been something he'd just had to take on faith, rather than pick apart and puzzle out.

He was telling the truth when he said he'd been nervous, but perhaps not in the way Zoey meant the question. It hadn't been the wedding—all those people there looking at him— that had worried him, or the fear of anything going wrong. And it definitely hadn't been the concept of marriage itself; the idea of spending the rest of his life with Grace had only ever made him smile.

No, he'd never been scared of committing

to Grace. But he'd been petrified of not being good enough to deserve her. Even now she was gone, the idea of not living up to the man she'd believed he could be kept him awake some nights.

Sometimes, he wondered if it was only Grace's belief in him, in what he could become, that kept him going after her death. That, and Zoey's blind determination to drag him out of the pit he'd buried himself in the moment the doctor had told him the news.

But that was him. It was all so different for Zoey. For her, it was the commitment she was terrified of. The idea of forever with one person.

Not that she'd ever told him that. But Grace had tried to explain it to him once, back when they were blissfully happy in their extended honeymoon period, and Zoey had just run out on her latest fiancé.

'It's not that she doesn't want to get married. She does, desperately, I think. It's just that after so many years of watching her parents perform the perfect How Not to Be a

Happy Couple *show, she's terrified of getting it wrong.'*

That had been three fiancés ago and now, sitting in a tiny storeroom of a luxury hotel, watching Zoey eye up the too-small window as a viable escape route again, Ash had to admit that his wife had been right. As usual.

Hardly surprising, he supposed. Grace had known Zoey better than anyone in the world. Almost as well as she'd known him.

And now he and Zoey were all that was left, trying to muddle through together. She'd literally picked him up off the floor after Grace was pronounced dead following a frantic ambulance ride from the scene of a multi-car pileup that stole three other lives. In return, he tried to be the best friend he could to Zoey, to make up for the much better one that she'd lost that day.

Some days he was better at it than others. He hoped today was a good day. Zoey looked as if she needed it.

And she was still waiting for him to explain his fears.

'It never occurred to me *not* to marry Grace.' Ash stretched out his legs along the table, turning so he could see Zoey as he talked. 'From the first moment I met her, she was my future. She was all I could think about.'

'I remember,' Zoey said, her voice dry. 'You had to be reminded that you'd actually met *me* that night too, when you both finally came up for air a week or so later.'

Ash winced. His eighteen-year-old self might not have been entirely aware of other people's feelings. But Zoey was smiling at the memory, so he figured he must have made up for it in the decade or so since then.

'So, why were you scared?' Zoey asked.

'Because…everything was so perfect. *Grace* was so perfect. I was scared I'd screw it up. That I wouldn't be enough.'

'*That* I get.' Zoey pulled her knees up against her chest, her bare toes with their sparkly aqua nails peeking out from under the hot pink dress. Ash spotted her high heels discarded by the door.

She looked about twelve, sitting like that.

Ash felt the familiar protective instinct rising up in him. Ever since Grace died, it had just been him and Zoey, looking out for each other. His parents, as much as they loved him, were generally more concerned with Ash's ability to perform his role in the family business than the state of his psyche, and Zoey's parents were worse than useless.

Which meant it was up to him to fix the latest twist in Zoey's romantic life.

Starting with figuring out which side of that window she *really* wanted to be on.

'Is that what this is about?' He scooted closer to sit beside her. The warm breeze from the open window brushed against the back of his neck. 'You're scared that you can't be what David needs?'

If anything, Ash thought it was the other way around. Of all her fiancés, David was his…second least favourite. Not that he was keeping a list. Well, not a written one.

But then, he and Grace had never thought anyone was good enough for their Zoey.

Zoey pulled a face. 'Not exactly. It's more…

I don't think that our marriage will be what either of us are hoping for.'

'But you didn't feel that way when you said yes to his proposal. Or when you told me that David was different, and that you'd absolutely go through with it and I wasn't to let you climb out of a window to escape getting married this time.'

'Hey! I told you. I've never climbed out of a window before.'

Ash raised an eyebrow to remind her that the window really wasn't the point here.

Because this was the part that Ash couldn't understand. When they'd had dinner a couple of weeks ago, when he'd been home in London between business trips, Zoey had been *so* certain, so sure of her love for David and their future together, that he'd resigned himself to boring dinners and holidays with the man for the rest of his existence. Because he wasn't losing Zoey in his life, whatever idiot she finally married.

He'd really thought that this time she'd go through with it.

But maybe that just meant he didn't know Zoey as well as he'd thought he did.

'Zoey. Tell me. What changed in the last two weeks?' he asked.

What always changes? Every damn time.

Zoey sighed as she tried to find the words. Find the reasons. How could she explain it to him when it didn't even make sense to her? It wasn't one thing that had changed. It was a hundred tiny things she'd finally noticed, all building on each other.

'Nothing. And everything.' She shook her head to try and clear the whirlwind of thoughts that seemed to have filled it since she arrived on the island. 'I really thought I could go through with it this time, Ash. That I could make it work. But then we landed here a few days ago to get everything ready for the wedding…and everything started feeling wrong.' Pit of her stomach wrong. Instincts telling her to run wrong.

She'd always trusted her instincts. Even when they led her into another engagement, or away from another wedding. At the time, they always seemed right.

'Everything?'

No. That wasn't fair to David. He was a good man. She loved him. Had loved him. One or the other.

'Well, little things, I guess. Like suddenly he wasn't happy with the ceremony plan and wanted to change it—even though it was what we'd both agreed *months* ago.'

'Last-minute nerves?' Ash suggested.

'Probably. But then I realised, all the changes he wanted to make, they involved me being with him all the time. Every single second. Even tonight, even though he *knows* my mother will freak out about it being bad luck.' And even though they were still doing the stupid abstinence thing the 'engagement counsellor' he'd hired had insisted on. Zoey hadn't even realised that engagement counsellor was an actual job, but David had been adamant that he wasn't taking any chances. Whatever the counsellor had suggested, he'd instantly implemented. Including the no sex for six weeks before the wedding rule.

No wonder they were both so tetchy and stressed.

'And why do you think that's bothering you so much?' Ash asked, sounding eerily like the relationship psychologist her ex-boss had introduced her to after her third near miss with marriage.

Really, with all these marriage professionals in her life Zoey would think she'd have the mental strength and tools to get through an actual wedding by now.

Of course, getting engaged to said relationship psychologist then calling it off three days before the wedding probably didn't help.

But she was getting side-tracked. This wasn't about past mistakes. It was about the one she might be about to make. Whichever way she jumped.

'Because…' Why *was* it bothering her? She was marrying the guy, so why would spending time together be a problem?

Then she realised. The reason behind that feeling in the pit of her stomach.

Ash had already told her, but she hadn't been listening. It was why she was on this stupid island in the first place.

'Because he's not doing it because he wants to be close to me. He's doing it because he wants to stop me running away.' God, he'd even planned the wedding for unfashionably early in the day to give her less time to bolt.

Zoey bit the inside of her cheek and stared down at her perfectly pedicured toenails. A waste of polish, really, if she didn't go through with the wedding. Not to mention all the time, money and energy that had gone into the planning. David might not need to worry about money right now—the company wasn't doing *that* badly—but Zoey had put her meagre savings on the line again for her dress and shoes, hair, beauty and all the rest. She couldn't ask her parents to pay for anything again. Not after all the times before. Even if they did seem strangely more enthusiastic about her marrying David than they had about anyone she'd been engaged to before.

She'd skipped a hen night this time—with Grace gone, it felt wrong anyway—and she'd only invited the hardcore friends and family who could make it through another one of her maybe-weddings. Ash, her aunt and uncle, a couple of cousins who were also friends. But David and his parents had invited *everyone*. She'd be letting a lot of people down.

But…

'It hurts to know he doesn't trust you.' Ash said the words softly, and for a moment Zoey could almost imagine that it was Grace, putting Zoey's own thoughts into words better than she ever could, just like she had since they were children.

Every time Zoey had shown up on Grace's doorstep as kids, with some story ready about why they urgently needed to hang out, Grace had just tilted her head and said, 'They're fighting again, right? Come in, come in.' Then they'd sat eating cookies or watching movies or anything to distract Zoey from what was going on at home.

'My home is your home,' Grace had told her when Zoey had run away at sixteen. And again at seventeen. Then she'd made sure they ended up at the same university, so Zoey wouldn't be alone when her parents flaked on her again, because they were too busy with their own misery.

Zoey had done what she could to keep her relationship with her parents going, but she'd always known that *Grace* was her real family. And Ash, once it became clear that he and Grace were a package deal.

She'd had visions of being part of their family for life. Christmases, birthdays. She'd be Auntie Zoey to their kids… She swallowed hard at the memory, knowing how close that one had been to coming true.

Before the crash. Before they all lost Grace for good, and the world had grown a little colder.

Zoey let her head fall to Ash's shoulder, taking comfort from the arm he placed around her. He might not be Grace, but he was still family.

And right now she couldn't afford to dwell in the past. She had to decide what to do about David.

'I know I'm a flight risk. I know I have form. And I know I'm proving him right at this very moment. It's just…if David doesn't trust me now, what if he doesn't ever? What if he's always just waiting for me to run? I can't live like that.'

'Nor should you,' Ash said. 'I can understand his reasons, but I can understand yours too.'

She looked up at him, into those strange, light blue eyes that stood out so clearly against his pale skin and black hair. 'So what do I do?'

'Well, that's up to you. Do you love him enough to convince him? Do you love him enough to take a chance? I mean, he obviously knew that asking you to marry him was risky. And, whatever steps he's been taking this week to make sure it happens, he was only doing it to make sure you go through with it.'

Zoey smiled. Although Ash was obviously trying to be fair to both sides of the story, playing devil's advocate, she could hear his distaste for David's methods in his tone.

Suddenly, they heard a voice in the corridor outside their store cupboard. 'Zoey? Come on, Zo, this isn't funny. My dad's waiting to give his speech. Where are you?'

'Decision time,' Ash whispered. 'What do you want to do?'

All at once a feeling of rightness settled over her.

'Get me out of here, Ash.'

CHAPTER TWO

SO THEY WERE RUNNING. Right.

Ash gave a sharp nod, then whispered, 'Stay here.'

Easing himself off the table, he opened the door to the cupboard an inch and peered out. David stood with his back to him, staring down two identical-looking corridors branching off from the main one at the far end of the hall.

Perfect.

Ash slipped through the door and closed it silently behind him. Then he took a few steps forward before calling, 'David! I've been looking for you everywhere.'

David spun around. 'Have you seen Zoey? She's been missing for fifteen whole minutes.'

If he'd sounded less irritated and more concerned, Ash might have felt guiltier about lying to him. Or if David had realised that Zoey had actually been gone for more than half an hour. As it was…

'That's why I was looking for you. She had a migraine so went up to her room to lie down.'

'A migraine? Tonight?' David pulled an exasperated face. 'Zoey doesn't even get migraines!'

Okay, now Ash barely felt guilty at all. 'She's had them since she was twelve. She had to take a make-up exam our last year at university when she missed one of her finals because of a migraine.' How could David not know that about her? Wasn't he supposed to be in love with her?

'Well, she's never had one in the eighteen months I've known her!' David snapped. Then he ran a hand over his hair, looking away. 'Sorry. I'm just…a little anxious right now.'

'Wedding eve nerves,' Ash said sagely. 'I remember them well. Look, why don't you go back and tell your guests what's going on.

I'm sure Zoey will feel much better in the morning.'

'Yeah. Yeah, you're right,' David said, already turning back the way he'd come. Ash smiled to himself. Sometimes, people just wanted someone else to tell them what to do. 'I could do with an early night, anyway. I'll go say goodnight then head up and check on Zoey. See if there's anything she needs.'

Okay, that wasn't *exactly* what he'd hoped for, but Ash would take it. It bought them a little time, at least.

'Great. I'll…see you back in there.' He waved a hand in what he thought was the direction of the bathrooms and hoped that David would get the hint.

He did. The moment David turned the corner towards the restaurant, Ash slipped back into the cupboard to find Zoey listening anxiously at the door.

'I definitely told him about the migraines,' she said indignantly.

'He forgot an important medical condition; you're skipping out on your absurdly expensive wedding,' Ash pointed out. 'I think you can call it even. And unless you want him following you, we need to go. *Now.*'

Getting out of the hotel, it turned out, was the easy part. Leaving behind the store cupboard and the too-small window, Ash guided them out through the kitchens instead. He'd spent enough of his formative years in hotels, when his father took him along on business trips, to know the ins and outs of most of them. And as a growing teenage boy he'd always, always found the kitchen first.

'Why didn't I think of this?' Zoey said as they weaved their way through the busy kitchens, apologising to the sous chefs and kitchen underlings as they went.

'Because you're only used to seeing hotels as a guest,' Ash pointed out. 'When you're staying somewhere as luxurious as this, people tend to forget that there's a whole world behind the scenes, working hard to make your holiday happen.'

'But not you?' Zoey's eyebrows were raised

and Ash recognised that expression all too well. That *You're a rich kid and you're lecturing me on how the other half live?* look.

'I spent a lot of time in hotels growing up,' he said. 'I got to know how they operate pretty well. And that was before I started working in the kitchens of one at the age of fifteen.'

Zoey stared at him incredulously as they burst through the final set of doors and into the only slighter cooler night air of the island. 'You? Ash Carmichael, heir to the Carmichael millions, worked as a hotel cook?'

'It's billions, actually. Or will be soon, if my father gets his way. And I was deputy washer-upper for three months before I was allowed anywhere near the food.' Ash scouted around the back of the hotel, making sure there were no loitering guests to see them run. 'My father is a firm believer in earning your place—even if you're born into it. I worked in every part of a hotel in the three years before I went to university, and after that I worked my way up through every department of Carmichael

Luxury Travel before I was allowed anywhere near the top offices.'

'Huh. Grace always said you worked hard, but she never mentioned all that.'

Ash shrugged. 'Why would she? It was just a job.'

And his job—and his money, for that matter—had always been the least interesting thing about him to Grace. Which was one of the reasons he'd fallen so hard and so fast for her. She'd loved him in spite of his name, not because of it.

'So, where do we go now?' Zoey looked out at the darkening skies, a nervous line marring the skin between her eyes.

A gnawing feeling of doubt settled in Ash's stomach. Was he doing the right thing, taking her away from this wedding? He'd promised her just two weeks ago that he'd make sure she went through with it. But even then he'd not felt entirely comfortable making that promise.

Watching her with David, he'd been worried. Or unsettled, perhaps. Nothing Ash could put a finger on, but just a sense of wrongness. Maybe it was the way that David's eyes never left her, especially when she was talking to other people. Or perhaps the way that they only ever said yes to engagements he wanted to go to, and arrived and left on his clock, not Zoey's.

Or maybe it was just that Ash didn't like him much.

Whatever it was, Ash had to admit that he was glad Zoey wasn't marrying him. If she'd gone through with it, there was an interminable future of boring dinners listening to David talking about how important he was, and how magnanimous, supporting Zoey in her little job at the gallery.

Yeah, he was definitely doing the right thing.

'The company has a villa on a private island, not far from this one. Freshly refurbished and awaiting inspection by yours truly next week. I even know where the spare key is hidden. We could borrow one of your guest's boats and be there before bedtime.' He nodded to the array of boats moored up at the hotel, ranging from small speedboats to large private yachts. Many of the wedding guests had decided to make a longer trip of the event and hired boats for the occasion to tour the region—relishing the excitement of island-hopping in the tropics instead of yachting around the Med for a change. Ash had been hoping for a chance to take a trip out on one of the boats anyway, so really he was killing two birds with one stone.

Actually, this all sounded like a pretty good plan for one he'd just come up with on the spur of the moment. Hopefully the villa had an equally luxurious drinks cabinet, and he and Zoey could wait out the wedding sipping cocktails by the pool before they headed back to face the music.

'Borrow a boat from somebody?' Zoey asked, sounding less enamoured of his plan. 'Doesn't that mean going back *into* the hotel we just escaped from and *telling* one of my guests that we're leaving? Kind of defeats the object, don't you think?'

'Well, I wasn't exactly going to ask,' Ash

admitted. He'd always found it better to seek forgiveness rather than permission in situations like these.

'So you want to *steal* a boat. From one of David's friends and family? Because I can't see that making me any more popular with them.' As if she thought running out on her own wedding wasn't going to achieve that on its own. Sometimes Zoey had no sense of priorities.

'No,' Ash explained patiently. 'We'll bring it back tomorrow. *After* the wedding that won't be. And we'll only borrow a small one, anyway. They probably won't even notice it's gone.'

'I'm not sure—' Zoey broke off abruptly as another voice filled the air. David's.

'Zoey? Are you out here?'

'Boat?' Ash whispered.

Zoey nodded. 'Boat.'

And then they ran.

As if she wasn't feeling guilty enough already, now she had boat theft to add to her weighty conscience.

Ash had commandeered a small yacht with surprisingly little trouble—one that had been hired, she had a feeling, by David's boss— which made Zoey wonder if he'd actually done this before. Funny, if she'd been asked this morning she'd have said that she knew everything there was to know about Ash Carmichael. After all, Grace had talked about him *incessantly* since the moment they met, so it was hard not to. And that was even before Grace died, and suddenly all they had was each other.

A tragedy like that brought people together. Made them close. Helped them know and understand each other in a way they never would have done, otherwise.

But somehow she still hadn't known that he'd worked in a hotel kitchen, or that he knew how to hotwire a boat, or whatever it was he'd done to steal this one.

It was a nice boat, Zoey decided, standing by the rail looking out at the rapidly receding island hotel where she wouldn't be getting married tomorrow. Stretching out from the main island itself was the long wooden bridge out over the water that led to twenty or so individual hotel suites on stilts, looking as if they almost floated on the waves.

It was an incredible place, Zoey had to admit. Under other circumstances, she'd be sorry to leave.

As it was…

She sighed and turned away, back to where Ash was steering the boat. And frowning. A lot.

'What's the matter?' she asked, drawing closer. 'Having second thoughts?'

He flashed her a smile. 'I'm pretty sure I'm supposed to be asking you that.'

Zoey considered, taking a reading on her internal feelings. A lot of guilt, as usual—and, really, who had a 'usual' for a situation like this?—but no regrets. No second thoughts.

She might regret letting her relationship with David reach this point, but not walking away. Her whole body sang with the rightness of that decision.

But that didn't explain Ash's frown.

'I'm absolutely fine. What's up with you?'

'Not me,' Ash said shortly. 'The weather.'

Zoey looked up and saw the sky ahead was a different colour to the sky behind. And, from Ash's expression, it wasn't just the usual gradients of colour of sunset in paradise.

'A storm?' she asked.

He gave a short nod. 'A squall, at least. Basically, out of the frying pan...'

'Into the dangerous weather systems.' Hadn't someone at the hotel said something about incoming weather that morning? Yes! They'd been talking about possibly having to bring the ceremony in from the beach into the hotel itself. David had been furious. She'd been so caught up in her own doubts and concerns she hadn't listened. She'd tuned out the way she always did when David was rude to someone he considered less important than himself. Which was basically everyone except his father. And her own parents, actually, which was probably why they liked him.

For someone who could be so sweet when it was just the two of them, he didn't go over so well with other people. Something else she should have considered sooner.

Maybe she was just an incredibly lousy judge of character. That would explain a lot.

But personal revelations didn't change the past. Or the squall in their future.

'I knew it was coming,' Zoey berated herself. 'I had a conversation with the wedding planner about it this morning—well, David did. But I was there. I should have remembered.'

'You've had a lot on your mind,' Ash said drily, but Zoey could feel the wind lifting her hair, and saw the way Ash gripped the boat's controls.

It was coming.

Looking over the side, Zoey could see the waves rising higher, crashing against the side of their boat. How on earth was she going to explain to David that she'd not only run out on their wedding but also destroyed his boss's boat in the process?

Maybe this was divine retribution. Fate taking its revenge for her messing up other people's lives and plans one time too many; taking control of her future for her, since she couldn't ever seem to stick to any of the decisions she made herself.

Maybe she deserved it.

'I should have checked the forecast before bringing you out here.' Ash's knuckles were white, Zoey realised, and his face pinched. Strain, fear or both? 'You should get down in the cabin. There's not much space down there, but it's a lot safer than up on deck.'

Or maybe fate was a load of bunk, and the future was hers to control.

'I'll stay here with you.' Zoey grabbed a hold of the railing beside Ash, planting her feet firmly on the deck. 'I mean, I have no idea how to drive a boat, so you'll have to tell me what to do so I can actually help you. But it's my fault we're out here. I'm not leaving you up here alone.'

Ash looked at her, his gaze steady despite whatever fear he was feeling. Zoey gazed back just as evenly, so he'd know she meant it.

Then the wind kicked up again and a wave

crashed into their side, making them both stumble a little.

'Okay,' Ash said, his eyes back on the water, his hands firm on the controls. 'We're not far from the island. Let's see if we can get there before this storm gets any worse.'

'We'll get there,' Zoey said with a confidence she wasn't sure she truly felt.

Fate could go hang.

What kind of idiot took a random boat out in these waters at night without checking the forecast? Ash berated himself mentally as he clung to his tenuous control of the boat. The waves crashed against the sides and Ash tried desperately to focus on the task in hand and not get distracted by images of his late wife giving him hell in the afterlife for getting her best friend killed.

With Grace gone, he was responsible for Zoey. It wasn't as if her parents had ever been able to let their own issues go long enough to care about her, and since the odds of her actually finding true love and settling down—at least long enough to get through a wedding reception—seemed to be getting slimmer, he was it. He was all the support she had left— and he was doing a lousy job of it so far.

The sky was growing blacker, the kind of doomed darkness that foretold of disaster to come. Maybe he should just have let her marry David after all. Sure, he'd probably have been throwing her a divorce party within six months, but at least she'd be alive to celebrate it, instead of dead at the bottom of the ocean.

He glanced to his left. Zoey was holding on tight to the rail beside him, obviously determined to stand by him—as much as he wished she'd just get to safety below. The waves weren't too big yet, but they were going to get bigger...

Then, suddenly, he got a glimpse of what he was looking for. Refuge. Safety. A fully stocked drinks cabinet, he hoped.

'There!' He risked raising one hand from the controls to point. 'Do you see that?'

Zoey leant forward over the rail, squinting into the distance and almost giving Ash a heart attack at the same time. 'Is that the island?'

'I hope so.' Ash braced himself and started to turn the boat. He'd studied the online maps and satellite footage well enough to know that the new acquisition was the nearest island to the one he'd recommended to David for the wedding. It had to be the right one. Hopefully. 'And if all else fails, it's *an* island.' Dry land had to be better than water right now.

As they grew closer, Ash could make out the outline of a wooden villa at the water's edge, the traditional stilts meaning it was half over the ocean and half on land. The roof looked to be the usual thatch, and he recognised the terrace layout from the photos of the recently acquired property he'd been looking at a few days before. This was the place they'd been searching for.

Best of all, there was even a mooring point for the boat. Ash just hoped it would hold overnight.

Once the wedding was over, Zoey was

going to want to leave again, after all. Well, eventually, anyway.

Getting the boat moored securely was a battle in itself as the threatened rain began to fall.

'Run up to the house,' he yelled at Zoey, his throat sore with the effort of getting her to hear over the storm. But Zoey shook her head, her wet hair whipping around her as she held on tight to one of the stern lines as he crossed them to tie up.

Stubborn. Just like Grace. No wonder they'd been such good friends.

Finally, finally, the yacht was as secure as he could make it. He'd just have to hope that was as secure as it needed to be. It was too late to do any more. The wind that had been steadily rising had reached a screaming pitch now, whistling and screeching through the trees and across the water. Looking back out to sea, Ash couldn't tell where the rain stopped and the waves started.

'Come on.' Grabbing Zoey's hand, he dragged her up from the small jetty towards the front door of the villa, already dreaming of what they'd find inside as he fumbled for the hidden key and tried to recall the security code he'd saved on his phone.

This place was perfect. Ash had read all the specs on the flight out. The villa was the newest jewel in his father's property crown, freshly refurbished to Arthur Carmichael's exacting standards. If a person had to take refuge from a storm and a potentially furious bridegroom, this was the spot.

He flung open the doors.

Zoey crashed into his back as he stopped, still on the threshold, and stared in.

Okay. So this place *would* be perfect. Once the renovation was *actually finished.*

'Can we get inside already?' Zoey asked. Ash could feel her shaking, shivering with cold as she pressed against him.

The storm was on them. There was no going back.

'You might wish you'd stayed and married David,' he muttered as he moved aside to let her in.

Zoey pushed past him, then stopped in the middle of what Ash assumed would be the lounge. Eventually.

'So, when you said that this place had just been refurbished...' She turned around slowly, taking in the room. Ash winced. Even in the darkness of the storm raging outside, he knew this didn't look good.

'I might have been a little optimistic.'

He tried to see the villa through her eyes. The half-built kitchen area off to one side. The random pieces of wood stacked up against the far wall. The windows still covered in tape but no blinds. The complete lack of furniture.

Zoey sighed. 'I suppose it's too much to hope for a fully stocked drinks cabinet, then?'

CHAPTER THREE

THERE WAS OFFICIALLY nothing luxury about the luxury villa Ash had promised her. Even without the storm raging outside, this would have been a disaster. As it was…

Well. They'd just have to make the best of it. After all, it had to be better than going back to the hotel and admitting to David that she'd tried to run out on their wedding but been driven back by bad weather and incomplete renovations. Besides, if she had to get on another boat again this lifetime it might be too soon for her seasick stomach.

Of course, she would have to. But not yet.

They had to make it through the night first.

'Maybe the builders have left some useful stuff lying around,' Zoey said. Although, looking around her, mostly they seemed to have left splintering wood and a lot of rubbish. 'Like blankets or tea or something. I'll go look.'

'And I'll go check the boat.' Ash didn't sound particularly excited at the prospect. 'Probably a better chance of finding things we need there anyway. Maybe even some dry clothes.'

Zoey glanced reflexively down at her beautiful strapless pink dress—now dark and sodden with water, streaked with sandy mud and clinging unflatteringly to her body. She imagined her hair must look even worse.

Good job that Ash had seen her in some seriously unflattering positions before, really—especially at university. At least he wouldn't be surprised. Or too horrified, hopefully.

'Wish me luck.' Ash flashed her a bright grin before pushing open the wide glass door and stepping out into the storm again.

'Good luck!' she called after him, but she doubted he could hear her over the wind. She tried to watch him go, but he was swallowed up by the darkness of the storm in no time.

Suddenly, Zoey felt very alone.

Well, that was what she'd wanted, wasn't it? To escape from the pressure and crush of all the people at the hotel, waiting for her to walk down the aisle in another white dress that didn't feel quite right, to marry a man who used to give her butterflies in her stomach but now gave her moths. Still unsettling but darker and somehow not right.

Oh, God, she'd done it again.

Her knees shaky, Zoey sank to the ground, her soaked pink dress pooling around her and leaving a puddle on the dusty, splinter-laden floor. Her hands twisted in the wet material as she tried to stop the tears threatening to spill over her cheeks.

Why was she *crying*, for heaven's sake? *She* hadn't been left at the altar, or the night before at least. *She* hadn't been abandoned, hadn't suddenly lost the future she'd imagined for her and David.

She'd chosen to run. Again.

She'd made her choice and now she'd live with it.

It was just… How could she have let this happen again?

The first time, with Kevin, it had been so hard. But she'd known it was the right decision. He told her he loved her, that he couldn't imagine his life without her, that he'd die if he couldn't have her…but he'd wanted her to give up her dreams of university, of a future career, to stay with him and see if he could make it as a rock star.

It had taken everything she had to hand him back his ring and walk away, but she'd never worried that she'd made a mistake. And whenever she'd missed him, she'd had Grace there to remind her why she'd done it.

The second time had been more complicated. She'd met Harry at university, not long after Grace and Ash became Grace-and-Ash. Maybe she'd been feeling left out, or maybe she'd just wanted something of the happiness they'd found, because it had been easy to fall into an echo of their relationship herself, with Harry. Except Harry wasn't Ash and she wasn't Grace. They weren't the perfect fit that their friends were, and they'd argued about almost everything.

They'd got engaged six months after they graduated, and Zoey had made it as far as addressing the envelopes for the invitations before she stopped and asked herself what on earth she was doing.

Grace and Ash had been waiting for her with a bottle of wine and a home-cooked meal at their new flat when she showed up, still gripping one of those damn invitations, and told them she didn't think she could go through with it.

Disentangling their lives together had been hard, and Harry hadn't understood what the problem was anyway, why she'd changed her mind so suddenly. But just one evening with Ash and Grace, seeing them clearly and realising everything they were that she and Harry weren't, had made up Zoey's mind for good.

She'd seen what marrying the wrong person could do to a couple—she'd lived with it growing up and, since her parents were apparently violently opposed to divorce, continued to witness it every time she went home. She hadn't understood, for years, what had kept them together, but she thought she did now. It was fear. Fear of scandal and gossip. Fear of losing the very comfortable lifestyle they had from the business they'd built up together—nothing on the scale of Ash's family business, of course, but enough that they didn't want to lose it in a bitter divorce battle. And, given how bitter their marriage had become, Zoey had no doubt that if either one of them ever caved and left, it would be horrific.

She didn't want that for herself, wouldn't let herself settle for a marriage held together by fear of how much worse things might be apart.

She wanted what Grace and Ash had, or it wasn't worth the bother of the fancy dress and the name changing.

She'd thought she'd found it over and over since then, with men who said they worshipped her, or men who promised to respect her, or even men who claimed they wanted them each to live their own lives, just together. But, in the end, something always changed.

There was always a moment when she looked at them and realised that, behind their words, they all wanted the same thing: to lock her in to a life that would no longer be her own.

Every time, it came down to the same problem. Marriage meant sharing a life, letting someone else have equal say in her decisions. It meant giving up control—and most of all it meant risk.

Risking everything on the promise that this guy would be different. That this man meant it when he said that he just wanted her to be happy—rather than *actually* meaning that he wanted her to be happy as long as it fitted in with what *he* wanted.

She'd seen how awful marriage could be if you made the wrong choice, and she wouldn't do that. If she ever finally made it to the altar and said 'I do' it would be because she was certain. That the risk was gone, because there were no doubts left.

Which seemed like a pretty impossible bar to reach.

Zoey sighed. Maybe she should just give up

on the whole idea of marriage. It wasn't as if she hadn't had the thought before. But every time she did…she remembered Grace's radiant happiness on her wedding day, and the way Ash had looked like the proudest, most joyous man in the world, and she knew it was possible.

True happiness, true love, was possible—and Zoey wanted it.

It just seemed she was going to have to keep looking to find it.

Slowly, she forced herself back to her feet, brushing the sawdust from her hands on her soaked dress before wiping away her tears. True love would have to take a back seat for a while. Right now she had bigger problems.

First things first. Survive the night. Then go back after the wedding was scheduled to happen and explain everything to David. Given the lengths he'd gone to in order to make sure she was there for the wedding, he presumably wouldn't be entirely surprised by her absence. In fact, he'd already know she was gone by now. Still, it wasn't a conversation she was looking forward to.

But she'd get through it, all the same. Then get back to London and her normal life as soon as possible.

Starting with finding somewhere to live. Oh, hell, she'd probably have to move back in with her parents, in the house and the village where she grew up, at least until she found her own place. And that was after she'd braved returning to David's flat to rescue her stuff. Well, it wouldn't be fun, but it would be necessary—and all steps towards a better future.

She could focus on her job, her future— what *she* wanted in life—and forget all about men.

After they made it through tonight.

With a firm nod to herself, Zoey set off to search the other rooms of the villa in the hope of finding some towels, blankets, food, and maybe alcohol.

Not necessarily in that order.

Ash ducked into the interior of the small yacht, the door slamming behind him in the wind. Water dripped from his hair, his clothes, his skin, all pooling around his very wet feet. It was just as well he hadn't taken the time to dry off while they were at the villa—it would have been a wasted effort. Right now, every inch of him was more water than man, and it was hard to imagine ever being dry again.

First priority: towels. And something waterproof to carry them in back up to the villa. Then maybe clothes.

He found a stash of beach towels in a cupboard under the bed and towelled off his hair as he hunted around for something to hold them while he dashed back to the villa. In the end, the best he could come up with was a bin bag from under the bathroom sink. At least, given the yacht's current owner, it was a high quality one, and Ash trusted it not to break.

There was no sign of anything to wear beyond a couple of towelling robes that wouldn't fit in his bin bag, so he made a mental note to come back for them once the rain had passed. As he placed them back in the cupboard, an image of Zoey wearing one, barefoot and fresh from the shower, popped into his head and he quickly shook it away. '*Not* the time for that sort of thought,' he muttered to himself. Zoey was his best friend. What would she say if she knew he was thinking of her that way—especially the day before she was supposed to get married?

Back on his quest, Ash raided cupboards and lock boxes for food—not much…all packaged and long-life—a torch and matches, a thick blanket, a two pack of toothbrushes and a tube of toothpaste, some tiny hotel-sized toiletries, and finally, in the last cupboard he checked, a bottle of single malt Scotch whisky.

Perfect.

It was only as he hoisted the bag onto his shoulder that he realised fully how ill prepared they'd been for running away. Zoey had left her handbag, her passport, everything at the hotel—including her high-heeled shoes. Did she even have her phone with her? He wasn't sure. Even if she did, reception had been so bad on the islands, he couldn't imagine there was any at all in a storm like this.

He hadn't stopped to grab his passport either, or anything that might have been actually useful, like an extra phone charger. All they had was the contents of his pockets, since he was pretty sure Zoey's dress didn't even have those, which amounted to his wallet, his phone—probably nearly out of battery, but hopefully still working after the rain—and his hotel room key.

That was it.

Had Zoey even thought about it before she'd tried to squeeze through that cupboard window? Had she considered what she was asking when she said, 'Get me out of here, Ash'? Probably not.

Grace had always said that for someone who acted on gut instinct so much, it was a shame that Zoey's intestines were such lousy decision makers.

Ash wondered now if that was right, though. Because Zoey didn't seem to be acting on the say-so of her gut, but her heart. And the heart, he knew, was a far more complicated organ. At least, when it came to relationships.

He liked to think he knew Zoey pretty well. She was the only person who truly knew how much he'd lost the day Grace died. Even if they'd never openly spoken about it.

Before, he'd always known that if there was ever a cause to choose sides, Zoey would be on Grace's, whatever the story. But now, now she was *his* best friend. The person he relied on, the one person he knew would always take his side.

Which was why he'd known, from the moment he'd found her trying to climb out of that window, that tonight wouldn't end the way he'd planned. Not that he'd honestly believed, deep down, that any pre-wedding night involving Zoey was likely to end the traditional way. Him buying David one last whisky in the bar, giving Zoey a hug and a pep talk and getting an early night, ready for the wedding first thing in the morning, had never really been on the cards. More likely sitting up drinking too late with Zoey, reassuring her that she could do this. He'd been prepared for some last-minute jitters.

He just hadn't expected those jitters to lead to them spending the night in a dilapidated villa on a deserted island in the middle of a storm.

When was the last time they'd spent the night together, just the two of them? Had they ever?

Probably in those first days after Grace's accident, although he didn't remember it well if they had. Before that it had always been the three of them. And since then, well, Zoey had a very uncomfortable sofa bed in her lounge he'd slept on a few times before he sold the house he'd shared with Grace and bought a new flat, without the memories. But somehow that felt very different from tonight. Maybe that was what had prompted his brain to imagine Zoey in a bathrobe and nothing underneath...

Tonight, they'd be huddled together avoiding the storm, sharing blankets and body heat, probably. With another woman, anything could happen.

But this was Zoey. Not only was she his

wife's best friend, but she'd literally just left a longstanding serious relationship. He shouldn't even be *imagining* anything like that.

Instead, he made himself remember the last time Zoey had called off an engagement at the eleventh hour. And the time before that, actually. Both times, she'd shown up at the house, looking distraught, and Grace had taken care of her. She'd listened, offered advice with no pressure to take it, tried to present different points of view, all without ever being less than one hundred per cent behind whatever Zoey decided to do next.

All Ash had needed to do was pour the wine and order the pizza.

He had a feeling that wasn't going to cut it tonight.

She was going to need to talk about things. That was how Zoey worked. And the only person she had to talk to was him.

I hope I can live up to your standards, Grace.

Except he was fairly sure he couldn't. In

fact, he had a sinking feeling he was going to screw this up magnificently—if he hadn't already achieved that by taking them to an abandoned villa on a stolen boat in the middle of a storm.

Ash hefted the bag up to his shoulder again and heard the whisky clank against something satisfactorily. At least he was still providing booze and food—his usual job.

As for the rest…he'd just have to wing it.

Zoey was his friend. She'd forgive him if he got it wrong. Right?

By the time Ash returned from the boat, Zoey had almost managed to make the villa habitable. Well, one small part of it, anyway.

She'd tried the lights first, but either the power was out because of the storm or it wasn't properly connected yet, because the villa stayed resolutely dark.

Using the torch on her phone—the only thing she'd grabbed from the table to take with her when she'd run—she'd explored the whole building, but most of it seemed in a worse state than the main room and with even less furniture, so she figured the open-plan central space at the front of the villa was probably the best place for them to set up camp for the night.

She'd found a large brush and tried to clear the worst of the sawdust and rubbish from the middle of the floor, and even discovered a couple of folding chairs that the crew presumably used for breaks, so set them out too. The biggest and best discovery had been the kettle, mugs and teabags on one of the half-built kitchen counters. Zoey hated to stereotype, but she had a feeling that old Mr Carmichael might have hired his favourite British builders for this job. No wonder they weren't in a hurry to get it finished if they got to hang out in paradise when they were done working for the day.

'Honey, I'm home,' Ash said drily as he shoved open the large glass doors again. Zoey turned. His voice was the only dry thing about him. Apparently the rain hadn't let up any since they'd arrived. Now she listened for it, Zoey could hear the raindrops hammering down against the windows and walls. The sound was so familiar already she'd stopped hearing it.

'What did you find for us?' She was hoping for food. Maybe vodka.

Ash threw her a towel. She supposed that was a start.

'Let's just say you're going to wish you'd waited until *after* the rehearsal dinner to run,' he said, towelling off his own hair then wrapping the towel around the back of his neck to catch the drips. 'But I did find this.'

He held up a bottle. Zoey grinned. She wasn't much of a drinker—beyond a couple of glasses of wine on occasional girls' nights or dinners out. Whisky definitely wasn't her favourite, but she supposed it *was* warming, and really, runaway bride beggars couldn't be choosers.

'Excellent. I found, well, not much. These chairs, and a couple of old blankets. Oh, and a kettle, so there can be tea in the morning.'

'Great minds...' Ash pulled a stash of teabags and some single serve UHT milk cartons from his pockets. 'That's all the important things covered. What do you want to do now?'

It turned out there really wasn't much *to* do in the middle of a storm on a desert island in a half-renovated villa. Drinking seemed categorically like the best option, especially considering the day she'd had, so they settled into their camping chairs and Ash distributed liberal amounts of whisky into the mugs Zoey had found. Zoey took a sip and pulled a face. Well, at least it seemed like the whisky would last them the night. She couldn't imagine drinking more than a tablespoon or two.

'So,' Ash said after a few quiet moments. 'As I recall from past experience, this is usually the point in the proceedings where you start talking.'

'Past experience?' Zoey raised her eyebrows. 'Have I forgotten all the other times we stole a boat together?'

'I was thinking more of all the other times you ran out on an unsuspecting fiancé.'

'Oh.'

Ash's gaze was measuring, as if he was watching to see which way she was going to jump. Zoey couldn't help but remember those other times he'd mentioned—how she'd always turned to Grace in times of crisis. About how Grace wasn't here to pick her up this time.

Tears burned behind her eyes. Maybe the whisky hadn't been such a good idea after all. Grace always said she was a total lightweight.

'I miss her, you know,' she said around the tightness in her throat. 'Every single day.'

Ash, to his credit, wasn't thrown by her non-sequitur. 'So do I.'

'Of course you do. She was your wife.' And he'd loved her so much. That had been obvious to anyone with eyes. 'Of course you're still grieving and stuff. But me…she was my best friend, and I don't have anyone else. But apparently I should be over this by now.'

Ash's face turned stony. 'According to who?'

'David.' Zoey took another sip of whisky, and then a bigger gulp. It burned her throat, but somehow that felt like a good thing, now. David would tell her that expensive whisky was wasted on her if she didn't enjoy it. But she didn't have to worry about what David thought any more.

The relief that flowed over her at the re-alisation was probably a sign that she really should have figured out the not-marrying-him thing sooner.

'In that case, I'm more pleased than ever that I helped you escape marrying him.' Ash scraped his chair across the floor to get closer to her, resting a hand on the plastic arm of her seat. Without thinking, she covered it with her own. 'You said it yourself, Grace was your best friend. You're allowed to mourn and grieve for her as long as you need to.'

It had already been nearly two years. Every morning, Zoey wondered if today would be the day she passed a full twenty-four hours without thinking about her friend, and all she'd lost. Without feeling the hole Grace had left in her life.

It never was.

'But you're wrong about one thing.' Ash turned his hand palm up under hers and gripped her fingers. 'You said you don't have anyone else. That's not true.'

'Isn't it?' Zoey raised her eyebrows as she looked at him, waiting for a joke about the barista she had a crush on at the coffee shop they went to together sometimes.

'No. You've got me.'

The sincerity in his gaze almost broke her. She knew, of course, that she'd sort of adopted him after Grace died—he'd needed someone, anyone, and she was the only other person who felt the loss of Grace so keenly.

But she'd never quite realised until now how much support and love Ash had given her in return. She'd imagined herself as more of an obligation to him—someone Grace would want him to check in on from time to time, to make sure she was okay—once the initial period of chaos and grief was over.

Looking into his eyes now, though, she knew it was more than that. *She* was more than that. More than just an old university friend he'd known for too many years and through too many wild nights out.

They were all each other had any more. Grace might have brought them together, but it was the loss of her that would keep them linked for ever.

She should have seen it sooner. Like when her heating had broken and she'd texted both David and Ash to moan, but David was in a meeting so just sent a sad face emoji text, and it was Ash who showed up with chocolate, blankets and the number of a recommended plumber.

Or her birthday, David had been out of town on business so sent flowers. Ash had been on the other side of the world, at some fancy resort in Australia, but he'd sent a basket with popcorn, wine and a Victoria sponge cake, complete with candles and a party hat, then video called her at six in the morning his time, just as she was getting home from work, so they could watch Netflix together and he could sing 'Happy Birthday' before she blew out her candles. He'd even worn a matching party hat to make her laugh.

Ash was the best friend she had in the world. And now, looking into his bright blue eyes, Zoey wondered how she'd never realised quite *how* good a friend he was. Maybe because she'd always been comparing him to Grace, or thinking of him as an extension of her old friend.

But he wasn't. He was Ash. She smiled, and he returned it with a bright grin of his own that made her throat go tight and her blood feel too warm. And suddenly Zoey realised that there was no one else in the world she'd rather be stranded with tonight.

CHAPTER FOUR

ASH LET GO of Zoey's hand and sat back in his rickety folding chair. That whisky must be stronger than he was used to, or at least faster acting, because he'd only had a couple of sips—not enough to affect him. Or maybe it was the after-effects of stress and excitement from the escape and the boat ride. Yeah, that was probably it. A delayed response to a near-death, or at least near-maiming, experience.

Nothing else would explain the strange feeling that just ran through his body as Zoey smiled at him. The one that seemed to fizz in his blood and brush across his skin with a feather touch.

A feeling he hadn't experienced in two long years.

The problem now wasn't imagining Zoey

in a bathrobe. It was the sudden flash of an image of her *out* of one that he couldn't shake.

Zoey. Best friend. Not someone to be imagining naked. Certainly not thinking about stripping that wet dress away from her skin…

He looked away, staring down at the whisky in his mug instead of at his best friend's face.

Zoey was a very lovely woman—he'd never denied that. But he'd never let himself think about her this way before—and he really couldn't afford to start now. She needed him as a friend tonight. That was all.

Maybe more alcohol would help.

Fortunately, it seemed Zoey was on the same wavelength, as she leant over to grab the bottle and top up both their mugs with considerably more liquor than he'd given them the first time.

What had they been talking about before? Something important. Something they should get back to…

Right. Zoey running out on her wedding. That definitely had precedence over any strange feelings he was experiencing.

'So, anyway. Talking. Do you want to? Talk about it, I mean?' Not his most elegant phrasing ever, but it seemed to get the intention across at least.

Zoey shrugged. 'What is there to say?'

What had Grace always done to draw Zoey out? Or did she just naturally talk to her in a way she didn't feel comfortable doing with Ash?

'Well, how are you feeling about everything? I mean, now we're on a completely different island from your fiancé, with no hope of getting back until after you're due to get married unless this weather breaks.' Even then, it might be a push. He wasn't sure how seaworthy that yacht would be after the storm had finished punishing it. The jetty he'd moored it at was rather more exposed than he'd like.

'Honestly?' Zoey said, still staring into her mug. 'Mostly I'm just feeling relieved.'

Ash's shoulders relaxed just a little at that. At least she wasn't regretting her decision. Because *that* would have been a problem he'd have no idea how to fix under the circumstances.

'He wasn't the right guy for you, Zoey,' he said softly.

She looked up with a sad half smile. 'They never are. That's the problem.'

'One of them will be, one day.'

'You can't know that.' Zoey shook her head, then took another gulp of whisky. 'Maybe there just *isn't* a right guy out there for me.'

'But maybe there is,' Ash countered. 'And if you stop looking, you'll never find him.'

She squinted up at him. 'Have you been reading self-help relationship blogs again?'

'No!' Well, not often, anyway. 'I just can't imagine someone as brilliant as you being alone for ever.'

Her cheeks turned a little pink at that, almost matching her still damp dress. It was funny, even drenched and bedraggled, shoeless and tipsy, she looked more beautiful than ever tonight. She always did, he supposed. He just hadn't ever let himself look before.

'What about you?' she asked, and the question threw him right back into the present with a jolt.

'How do you mean? I'm fine. Wet, but fine.' The towels hadn't been nearly good enough. He really wished he'd been able to bring the towelling robes as well—the stress it might have put on his imagination notwithstanding. At least then they could have got out of their soaked clothes.

Let me help you out of that wet dress...

Ash choked on a mouthful of whisky as the image of him undressing Zoey flashed through his mind.

Really not the time.

'I mean, do you think there will ever be anyone else for you? After Grace, I mean?'

Ash put down his mug. What did it say about him that the idea had hardly even crossed his mind in the last two years?

'I... I don't know. I mean, it's hard to imagine it. I can imagine dating, maybe even sex with someone else.' Hell, he'd been doing that right here, right now, at the most inappropriate time ever, curse his imagination. 'But the idea of loving someone else. Marrying them. Making a life with them…that's… I just can't see it. Literally. I can't picture it in my mind. You know?' When Grace had died, he'd lost not just his wife, but his whole future. The family he'd hoped to have one day was gone for ever.

'I know,' Zoey said sadly. 'That's the problem I have. I can see myself in the future, with a family, a home, a happy life. And there's always a vague figure in the background— a husband or partner or whatever. But I can never quite *see* him.'

'Not even when you're getting ready to walk down the aisle to meet him?'

Zoey shook her head. 'I guess I always think it'll come together. That everything will come into focus once I have that dress on and the ring on my finger. But then it comes to the day and the picture still isn't there. I can't ever see how to get from where I am to where I want to be.'

'So you *do* want to get married, then?' Ash asked. Grace had always said that Zoey wanted a happy marriage but, given how many times she'd walked out on the possibility of one, Ash had to wonder. 'Are you sure that marriage isn't just something you think you're supposed to want but don't really? I mean, it isn't for everyone. It doesn't have to be.'

'I know that.' Zoey looked up, straight into his eyes, and he felt a jolt go through him at the intensity of her gaze. 'But I want it. I want the whole thing—true love, marriage, a happy-ever-after. I want that more than anything.'

And he knew she meant every single word.

She'd never told anyone this before—except Grace. She let people believe that it was fear of commitment that made her run, let them think she just had the worst relationship style in the world. She never let on that it was only *because* she wanted that happily-ever-after so badly that she kept running out on it.

Zoey knew how much it was worth, how much it mattered—and how much it could hurt to settle for anything less. And that was why she couldn't marry anyone if she had a shred of doubt about how it would end up.

People wouldn't get it, she knew, which was why she didn't talk about it. The few times she'd discussed true love and happy ever afters with other people—usually after drinks—the reactions had not been encouraging.

Most people tended to fall into one of two camps. On the one side were those who believed that true love and soulmates were a fallacy, probably put about by greeting card companies and romance novelists. On the other were those who told her that marriage took work, that no one was happy all the time and that she should be grateful for what she had.

In the end, they were both saying the same thing, Zoey had realised eventually.

Stop wanting so much.

But she *did* want. And it wasn't about the ring or the ceremony or the big party or whatever happened next. It was about having the right person next to her when it happened.

And maybe some people truly believed that soulmates didn't exist—or maybe they were just saying it because they hadn't been lucky enough to find theirs. But Zoey knew for a fact that soulmates were real.

Because she'd watched Ash and Grace fall in love.

Even now, she used them as a benchmark. She thought back to how they'd been in their early days together and tested each of her own new relationships against the memories. And, for a while, they'd often match up—or perhaps she'd just convince herself that they did, half through optimism and half through desperation.

But there always came the point where she had to admit the truth to herself—her relationships were never that picture-perfect, soft-focus, tumbling headlong into love that she'd seen Ash and Grace manage at eighteen.

That wouldn't stop her looking, though.

'I want what you had with Grace,' she whispered, looking down at the mug in her hands. 'More than anything, that's what I want. That perfect happiness.'

There was an awkward silence emanating from the other folding chair. When she risked looking up, Ash's expression was conflicted, as if he couldn't decide whether or not to say what he was thinking.

'What?' she asked.

'Zoey, you know how much I loved Grace. And how much she loved me. But that doesn't mean things were perfect all the time. I mean, we fought, just like any couple. Stupid fights over whose turn it was to put the bin out, or whose fault it was we slipped into our overdraft that month. And bigger things too, like whether we should move house, or when we should have kids.' His voice caught on the last word and Zoey felt guilty for even making him remember how much he'd lost. She started to interrupt, to tell him he didn't need to say this, but he shook his head and continued. 'If I'd known how things would end, believe me, I'd take back every single one of those arguments and let her get her own way every time.'

'No, you wouldn't.' Zoey felt a small smile tugging at her lips. 'Because that's not who you two were together. Of course I know it wasn't perfect happy families every second. That's not what I mean.'

'Oh? Then what *do* you mean?'

Zoey cast around for the right words. 'When you two argued, it was because you were working something out between you. You were building a partnership—one that was far deeper and more important than the bins or the overdraft, but those things still had to be dealt with. Every row you had, it brought you closer together. Closer to the people you wanted to be for each other.'

Ash looked a little stunned at her words. Zoey allowed herself a small smile. Had he really never thought about how the two of them looked to the outside world? The perfect couple, made to be together. Hashtag relationship goals, for sure.

'It wasn't…it wasn't ever about being perfect, you know. I just loved her so much I wanted her to be happy. For us to be happy together.'

'And you'd do anything to get there, I know. Sadly, I think you've ruined me for other men. The pair of you, I mean,' she added hurriedly. 'As a couple.' The last thing she needed was for him to get the wrong idea now. Even if a few impure thoughts had flashed through her head as he sat there, hair wet and shirt clinging to his body. Not that she was admitting to them.

'Right. Sorry…what?'

Even as she looked up at his adorably confused face, Zoey could feel a blush rising to her cheeks.

'I just meant, I want what you and Grace had. I know that sort of love is possible and I'm not willing to settle for anything less. That's all.'

Ash shook his head. 'So it's *my* fault you keep walking out on your weddings? Please, don't ever let any of your ex-fiancés hear you say that.'

'Well, yours *and* Grace's,' Zoey corrected, but that only made him laugh.

'I'm not sure if that makes it better or worse.'

Suddenly restless, Zoey jumped to her feet, cradling her mug against her chest as she paced to the window to watch the rain and the dark. 'Do you think I'm crazy? I mean, you wouldn't be the first person to suggest that my approach to love might actually qualify me for some serious free therapy.'

'How could I? I mean, it's my marriage that you're basing your theories on. It's just…'

'You can't see anyone falling for *me* like that,' Zoey finished for him. 'Don't worry, it's not like I haven't had the same thought myself.'

'No.' Suddenly, he was right beside her and she stopped staring out at the rain to turn towards him as he grabbed her hand. 'That's not what I was going to say at all.'

Zoey stared up into Ash's strange light blue eyes and wondered at the chain of events that had brought them to this moment. She couldn't, wouldn't have predicted any of them. In fact, she'd have avoided or stopped most of them if she could.

But now she was there, she couldn't imagine her life going any other way.

She was meant to be here, now; she could feel it in her bones.

Even if she had no idea why.

'What were you going to say?' Zoey asked, the words coming out strangely breathless.

Ash gave a sad smile. 'Only that I know how lucky I was. How rare it is to find the one person you're truly meant to be with. I honestly hope that you do, and when it happens I'll be there to catch the bouquet.'

'But?' There was always a but, in Zoey's experience.

'No buts, not for you, anyway.' He shrugged. 'But, whether I catch the bouquet or not, I know it won't happen for me again. The odds are too astronomical. And I'm like you. I know what true love feels like now so I can't accept anything less.'

It wasn't new information. He'd already told

her he couldn't imagine loving again, after Grace. But somehow, standing with her hand in his in the darkness, Zoey felt his words deep in her heart, like gouges.

Which was ridiculous. She'd literally never thought of Ash that way—not as someone she could fall in love with. Of course she'd noticed he was gorgeous—that kind of thing was hard to miss. And there had been one or two dreams that had made their next get-togethers very uncomfortable for her. But he was Grace's. Always had been, always would be. Zoey had never forgotten that for an instant.

She pulled her hand away from his. It was just the emotion of the day—the craziness and the changes—getting to her. That was all.

But then Ash grabbed her hand back again and held it against his chest, and her treacherous heart skipped a beat.

'Zoey...' Ash trailed off, uncertain of what he even wanted to say. Just something. Anything that would wipe that hopeless look from her face.

This was why she needed Grace. He couldn't even get further than her name. What kind of comfort was that?

'It's okay, Ash.' Zoey started to pull away again, but instinctively Ash clung on.

There was something in this moment. Something important. And he knew, suddenly, that if he didn't tell her now what her friendship meant to him, he never would. And Zoey deserved to know.

'No. I want to tell you… I wouldn't be here without you.' He poured all the sincerity he felt into the words.

Zoey laughed in response, which wasn't quite what he'd intended. 'Well, no, Ash. If it weren't for me and my ridiculous inability to get married, you wouldn't be stuck here in some mystery island renovation project in the middle of a storm.'

'That's not what I mean either.' Taking the mug from her, he put it down on the half-built counter and took both her hands in his.

'I mean, after Grace. If it hadn't been for you, pulling me up, talking me through it, making sure I got out of bed in the mornings, I don't know if I'd have been able to keep going.'

'You would,' Zoey said, with more certainty than Ash felt. 'You know how furious Grace would have been if you didn't.'

'That's true.' His wife had been a stern believer in living your best life, even if the circumstances sucked. She never gave up on anything—until that last, awful ambulance ride. 'But you made it easier. You made it seem possible.'

Zoey shrugged, her gaze sliding away from his. 'I didn't do much. I had no idea *what* to do. For weeks, I just kept hoping it was a mistake. That the universe meant to take me instead of her.'

Her matter-of-fact tone made Ash's blood run cold. As much as he would give to have his wife back—up to and including his own life—he couldn't wish away Zoey's in such a manner.

'You know, you're the only other person

who knows how much was taken from me that day. Not just Grace, but—' He broke off, unable to say it.

'The baby,' Zoey whispered for him, and he nodded.

Grace had just turned twelve weeks pregnant; he or she had still been a tiny, perfect embryo. Zoey was the only other person Grace had told, wanting to wait until after the scan to make a big announcement. And afterwards, Ash hadn't been able to bring himself to mention it. But knowing that she knew, that his child was real for someone other than just him, that helped, a little.

'You knew what I'd lost. But still, you reminded me that the world was worth living for,' he said softly. 'Every day, you showed me everything that was still with me. From a sunny day in the park, to the best ice cream from that place by the canal, to just having a great friend to watch movies with on a Sunday afternoon. You never told me to smile, or to be happy. You were just there. Spending time with me, expecting nothing, but reminding me every single day that the world went on, and that was a good thing.'

Zoey stared up at him, her eyes wide and amazed. He didn't blame her. Ash wasn't entirely sure where those words had come from, either. But now he'd said them, he knew they were absolutely true.

'I want to do the same for you.' He pulled her close by their joined hands, until their hands were the only thing separating the two of them. 'Zoey, you've been my constant friend and support ever since that day at the hospital, and I'm not sure I've been anything close to the same for you.'

'You have!' she protested. 'Remember the long-distance Netflix binge on my birthday? With the cakes and the hats?'

Ash smiled, despite himself. 'I do.' Grace had always made such a big deal about people's birthdays—especially Zoey's. She always said it was because Zoey deserved a fuss, and no one else in her life was going to give it to her. When a reminder popped up on the electronic calendar he and Grace had shared, a week before the big event, he'd realised that, without Grace there, Zoey's birthday could go unmarked altogether. For some reason, it hadn't even occurred to him that David might celebrate it properly—and, of course, he hadn't.

So Ash had taken up the challenge. Even if he had to be thousands of miles away on the day, that was no excuse not to celebrate.

That was what Grace would have said.

'That was just a tiny drop in the ocean compared to all the things you've done for me,' he pointed out.

Zoey looked shyly down at their clasped hands. 'Maybe. But it meant the world to me.'

Releasing one hand from her fingers, Ash tucked it under her chin, forcing her to look up at him. 'You are worth far, far more.'

He could see incredulous disbelief vying with hope in her eyes. Ash wished he could convince her. Could show her that she was worthy of so much more than the men who just wanted a ring on her finger, but not the full Zoey experience. Worth more than countless last-minute escapes at the altar. Worth more than a long-distance video call and some cake on her birthday.

He wanted to show her that she was worth *everything*.

'There's no one in the world I'd rather be stranded in paradise with.' He'd meant it as a joke, something to lighten the mood, but it didn't come out that way. Instead, it came out serious, heavy with meaning. The words reverberated around his chest, surrounding his heart, filling him with a feeling he couldn't quite identify. And from the way Zoey bit her lower lip, she felt it too.

'Me either,' she whispered, her gaze never leaving his for a moment.

And then…then it was as if his mind shut down altogether and his body took over. Or maybe, maybe it was his long-ignored heart.

All Ash knew was that suddenly he was kissing Zoey Hepburn. And it was glorious.

CHAPTER FIVE

THE STORM HAD stopped.

As Zoey raised her aching head from her pillow, the first thing she noticed was the lack of rain hammering on the roof and windows. The second was the blazing sunlight that was making her eyeballs throb.

The third was that her pillow wasn't a pillow.

Oh, I've really done it this time.

Her head hurt too much to process the sight of Ash Carmichael lying beneath her, a rough towel draped across his hips and the rest of him probably—*definitely*—naked.

Naked. Her best friend was naked.

And, oh, hell, so was she.

Okay, this might be her biggest screw-up yet. Forget running out on multiple fiancés.

This was the act that was going to send her to hell.

She had slept with Grace's husband. Her body, through the whisky hangover, was very sure about that much, at least. And as she sat, stunned, looking down at the perfection of his torso, the sweep of his dark eyelashes against his pale cheeks, his tousled black hair, all sorts of other memories started coming back.

Memories that made her chest tight and her cheeks red.

Memories that, under literally any other circumstances, would be very fond ones. Ones to relive in private, later. Ones to keep her warm on cold winter nights.

As it was...

'Oh, hell, I slept with Grace's husband,' she whispered, then clapped a hand over her mouth to try and keep from waking him. The last thing she needed was an awake and alert Ash before she'd figured out what the hell she was going to do next.

Grabbing the second towel they'd been

using as a blanket, which had been thrown aside at some point during the night—she wasn't thinking about *which* point—Zoey wrapped it tightly around herself and tucked in the ends so it covered everything important. Somewhere, her pink dress must be lying abandoned, but even if she could find it Zoey wasn't sure how she could ever wear it again without remembering Ash stripping it from her body with long, capable fingers...

No. She wasn't thinking about that.

She was thinking about how to fix this.

Zoey paced to the window, rested her sore head against the cool glass and tried to focus.

This was a mistake. They must both know that, surely. And when Ash woke up he'd be embarrassed and confused, just like she was. They'd laugh about it, put it all down to the whisky and the drama of the storm, then they'd make a pact never to mention it again. Easy.

Except not mentioning it wasn't the same as forgetting.

And she knew all too well that the whisky

wasn't responsible for what had happened last night. Not on her part, anyway.

She'd wanted him—wanted Ash to kiss her, to touch her, to make love to her, long before the whisky had taken effect. Alcohol had just given her brain permission to take what she wanted—had helped her forget all the reasons she shouldn't.

Guilt swamped her, heavy as a raincloud fit to burst. It wasn't just Grace she'd betrayed, it was her friendship with Ash too. Never mind that Grace was dead. Sleeping with Ash now…it undermined everything they'd had before. Suddenly, she couldn't look back at all those happy memories of the three of them without wondering if the lust and passion of last night was lurking there too, under the surface.

If she'd always been thinking of this, planning it even, all along—however subconsciously.

Had she?

She didn't think so. But then, she'd never have thought she'd sleep with Ash at all, let alone the night before she was supposed to marry someone else.

Slipping out through the bi-fold doors that opened onto the veranda over the ocean, Zoey gulped in the fresh sea air to try and clear her head. Closing the door as silently behind her as she could, she moved across to sit on the edge, her feet trailing just above the water, so the odd wave lapped against her toes.

She needed to think. To figure out what the hell had just happened—and why.

Leaning back on her hands, she let the morning wind ruffle her hair and awaken her skin. The last vestiges of the previous night's storm still lingered in the air—a cooler, fresher breeze than she was used to out here in the Indian Ocean, and the tang of salt in her mouth with each breath. The waves were higher too—not the crashing, terrifying crests of water they'd experienced sailing in the night before, but enough to show that nothing was calm, that it wasn't all over yet.

In fact, Zoey was rather afraid it might only be beginning.

Alone on the deck, she couldn't resist the urge to relive the night before in her mind. After all, how was she going to fully understand what had happened—or figure out what she should do next—if she didn't fully examine what she'd done? The fact that her heart-rate picked up at the memories was just an aside.

It had started with that kiss.

That stupid, ill-thought-out, spur-of-the-moment, mind-blowing kiss.

Zoey had never spent much time before imagining what it would be like to kiss Ash—she hadn't needed to. Grace had described it in absurd detail the first time she'd kissed him.

But the kiss Zoey had experienced was nothing like that decade-old description.

'It was perfect, Zoey,' Grace had said, bouncing a little on her bed in their tiny shared university flat. *'Like flowers and white wine and romance and rose petals. Not too much—you know, some guys can just get a little over-enthusiastic with their tongue?'*

Zoey had nodded at that. She knew.

'But Ash... He was gentle and careful and responsive and...'

She'd sighed, a dreamy look on her face, and Zoey had thought she understood exactly what she meant.

But that wasn't the kiss that Zoey had received last night.

When Ash kissed her there were no rose petals or romance. No holding back or being gentle.

But if she was honest with herself that had only made it better. Hotter.

Her eyes fluttered closed as she remembered.

Even as his lips had brushed hers for the first time, she'd felt her blood heating up. That first touch had sent her wild—and it seemed to have the same effect on Ash too. Within moments, his hands were at her back, holding her closer as his mouth worked over hers.

He'd pulled back for a half second, just long enough to meet her eyes and murmur, *'Okay?'* But the moment she'd nodded he'd been on her again, a drowning man who needed her kisses to survive.

Zoey had to admit it had been hot as all hell. But a huge mistake.

Her eyes snapped open and she focused on the cool blue of the ocean, on the breeze against her skin, reminding her treacherous body of all the reasons why sleeping with Ash was the worst idea possible.

One: I just ran out on my own wedding. Again.

Two: I might technically still be engaged to David. Hell, she was still wearing his ring. Shame burning her cheeks, she tugged the diamond solitaire from her finger, realised she had nowhere safe to put it, and shoved it back onto her right hand instead as a compromise.

Three: he's my best friend's husband. That was the biggie, of course. It didn't seem to make any difference to her heart or head that Grace had been dead for two years. It still felt like the worst and grossest betrayal.

Four: everything is different now.

They'd grown so close as friends. Ash was

the only person she knew who was always in her corner. And now? She'd ruined that.

No, *they'd* ruined it. This was very much his fault too.

Zoey sighed, and tried to think her way out of the muddle her brain was in. But, before she could get further than *We need to fix this,* the bifold doors opened again and Ash stood there, wearing just his trousers from the night before, topless and gorgeous, his hair mussed from sleeping on the floor and his eyes knowing and heavy.

Oh, God, now what do I do?

Ash's first thought upon waking was, *We need to do that again. Soon.*

Then his brain—and his hangover—caught up with his libido, and he winced.

Cracking open his eyes—slowly—he took in his surroundings. Mid-refurbishment luxury villa. Hard and chilly tiled floors against his bare arse where the towels they'd lain on had shifted in the night. Wide glass windows and doors exposing him to the world outside, except for the towel laid across his middle, just about covering his modesty.

No Zoey.

Really, apart from that last part, he'd had worse morning-afters. But not for a long time—not since before he'd married Grace.

Grace.

Guilt flooded him with a heat that beat any tropical summer, and he sat up slowly as he took stock of what he'd done.

For the first time in two years, Grace hadn't been his first thought on waking. It wasn't that he'd forgotten her, of course, just that the memory hadn't been top of his brain the moment his eyes opened.

After she died, for the first few months, he'd often wake up expecting her to be lying beside him. Those mornings were even worse than the others—the ones where he woke up with the knowledge of her death already heavy on his chest. At least with the second sort he didn't have to deal with hope leaving him all over again.

But this morning—this morning he'd thought

about last night first. And that had never happened before.

Wrapping the towel more securely around his waist, he stood up, wishing he'd raided the first-aid kit on the boat for some painkillers.

Where was Zoey? It wasn't as if she could have gone far, unless she'd been desperate enough to try and sail the boat back alone, which seemed unlikely. Not least because the storm had probably battered the little yacht enough that it would need some attention before it could go anywhere. Also, because she didn't know how.

So that meant she was still on the island somewhere, and they were going to have to talk about it.

I slept with Zoey Hepburn.

God, he was an idiot. What kind of guy seduced a woman who'd just run out on her wedding? He was pretty sure that wasn't in Grace's handbook for How To Look After Zoey. Or wouldn't have been, if she'd ever written such a thing.

He wished, not for the first time, that Grace

had written him a guidebook on how to live life without her. Maybe then he wouldn't be screwing up the only real friendship he had left so damn badly.

Okay, so. First step. Talking.

No, first step—clothes. Otherwise nothing about this was going to get any easier.

Tugging on his suit trousers, he headed for the large glass doors that led out to the veranda. As he opened them, he spotted Zoey, sitting on the deck just out of sight from the villa, her feet dangling over the water.

She turned to look at him as he approached and he saw everything she was feeling in her eyes. Zoey had always been an open book, unable to stop her every emotion showing on her face. He studied her, to get a read on how she was feeling.

There was guilt there, unsurprisingly. And confusion and…fear?

Ash's insides tensed at the last one. Why was she afraid? And what sort of terrible friend was he to have left her feeling that way?

Mild panic setting in, he quickly ran over

the previous night in his head. They might both be thinking better of it this morning, but in the moment she'd wanted it as much as he had, hadn't she? He'd checked. Repeatedly. With every step forward they'd taken.

Her responses—physical and verbal—had been enthusiastic enough for him to relax a little. Whatever she was afraid of, it wasn't his behaviour the night before, he was sure.

'Good morning.' His voice came out scratchy from last night's whisky and he cleared his throat as he sat down beside her— close enough for friends, not so close as to spook her.

'Hey.' She gave him a small half smile. 'Sleep well?'

'Surprisingly, yes,' he replied. 'Given the lack of comfort and the luxury I was promised here.' Of course, the vigorous exercise and whisky before bed had probably helped with that. But he didn't mention it. Even though she had to be thinking it too.

Could he blame the whisky? They'd certainly drunk enough of it. But Ash knew himself too well for that. Whisky might lower his inhibitions, but there wasn't enough in a whole bottle to make him do something he didn't want to do anyway.

And, oh, God, he'd wanted Zoey. If he was honest with himself, he still did. Even hungover and regretting putting their friendship on the line—it didn't change the fact that he saw her in a new light now. He knew how it felt to kiss her, to touch her, to feel her. And that wasn't something any amount of alcohol could wash away.

They sat in awkward silence for a long moment, looking out over the water as sea birds swooped low and waves crashed high.

'Do you think the boat is okay?' Zoey asked suddenly. 'I mean, for us to sail back this morning?'

'I'll go take a look when my head's stopped pounding so much,' Ash replied. His head hurt a little more just thinking about it.

'What will we do if it's not okay?' There

was panic rising in her voice now, Ash could hear it.

'You mean, how will we explain it to the guest who hired it? They'll have insurance, Zo, don't worry. And if there's a problem, I'll pay.' He used his most soothing voice, trying to calm her, but somehow every word only seemed to make her more agitated.

'I mean, how will we get off this island!' She jumped to her feet. 'I need to get back there, Ash. Now.'

He blinked. 'Back to… David?' *Surely* she didn't mean what he thought she meant.

'The wedding is supposed to start in two hours,' she said. 'If the boat is okay—'

'You could get back and marry the man you already told me you'd be unhappy with?' Ash raised his eyebrows. 'Zoey, sit down. Let's talk about this.'

She shook her head, her dark hair whipping around her face in the wind. Wrapped in a towel that barely covered the tops of her tanned thighs, she looked wild, unpredictable.

And gorgeous. Utterly, utterly gorgeous.

Ash looked away and waited for her to sit. She didn't.

'I don't want to talk. I want to get back to where I'm supposed to be.' Her eyes were wide and wild too, he realised when he looked back. As if control was slipping from her grasp and she wasn't even trying to catch it.

'You're not supposed to marry David today,' Ash said calmly.

'What? So now you're a big believer in fate and destiny? And you've decided mine?' She threw the words at him, and he wondered if she knew how much they stung.

'You know I'm not,' he said softly, remembering the people who'd told him, after Grace's death, that all things happened for a reason, that God had a plan.

He'd known they were trying to offer comfort, which was the only reason he hadn't screamed at them that whatever plan this was, he hadn't agreed to it. That any God who had a reason for taking his wife and unborn child from him had better start explaining Himself pretty damn fast.

Sometimes, there were no reasons. And talk of fate and destiny only tried to hem people in to decisions they shouldn't be making, in his opinion.

Zoey's expression turned contrite. 'I'm sorry. I just…'

She trailed off, so he tried to find the words for her. 'You're scared and confused. Just like me. Which is why we should talk.'

But Zoey shook her head again. 'I can't. I'm sorry.'

Then, with a whirl of hair and towel, she'd turned and gone, disappearing back into the house and slamming the door shut behind her, before he could even think of following.

Ash stared out at the water.

'Well. That could have gone better.'

Yes, fine, okay, so technically she was running away again. At least she had a *theme*. Like, a personal calling card. If you wanted her, she was already gone.

And Ash had only wanted to *talk* to her. Imagine if he'd wanted to *marry* her.

Don't think about it. Don't think about it.

Too late. The idea was already there in her head. Festering.

Quickly, Zoey dragged on her still damp pink dress, ignoring the streaks of dirt from the boat, the storm and the sawdust, and let her towel drop to the floor. She needed real clothes to face today, however ruined they were.

Matches my mood.

Without looking back to see if Ash was following—*please don't let him be following*—she dashed out of the front door of the villa, away from the veranda and towards the beach.

'I need to go check on the boat,' she told herself under her breath as she marched away from the villa—away from *him*. 'See how bad the storm damage is to the island too. It's the responsible thing to do.'

And just because she hadn't been the responsible one at any point up until now, that didn't mean it was too late to start, did it?

Her determination and sense of righteousness lasted until she reached the edge of the sea and realised she'd stormed off in the wrong direction for checking on the boat and had no idea what the island had looked like *before* the storm hit.

Gathering her dusty and windswept hair into a knot at the base of her neck, she pulled it through itself until it stayed in place, held by dirt and sea salt, she supposed. Then her wobbly legs gave way and she dropped down to the sand, her legs folded under her.

She'd thought—she'd hoped—that they'd look at each other this morning and laugh. Brush away the events of last night as a drunken mistake, one that wouldn't affect their friendship in the least.

But then she'd seen him again and known, without a shadow of a doubt, that however *he* felt about their indiscretion, she wasn't going to be able to brush it aside or forget it at all. Ever.

His touch was burned into her skin. His kisses owned her brain now—she could think of nothing else when she saw his lips. And his body… How had she never touched it before? Been touched by it. Felt it sliding against hers—

Because he was married to someone else. Because he *loved* someone else. Still, even now. Grace was it for him—he'd told her as much.

So what was the point in pretending otherwise? In imagining—even for a moment—that things could be different.

What was wrong with her that a man kissed her and her thoughts instantly went to white dresses and diamond rings?

'It doesn't have to be all or nothing, Zoey,' Grace had told her once. *'You can have love without marriage, the same way you can have marriage without love. And not every potential relationship has to go the distance. Some are only meant for right now.'*

And some could only ever be one stupid, drunken night of passion.

Because, whatever Grace said, Zoey *wanted* that for ever kind of happiness. And Ash was the last person who could give that to her—because he'd already had it. Lightning didn't strike twice and all that.

And, even if it could, she couldn't live with always knowing that she was second choice, that she'd never live up to Grace's memory, whatever she did. Grace had been a ridiculously hard act to follow as a friend. But as a lover? A wife?

'There's no one in the world I'd rather be stranded in paradise with.'

Ash's words came back to her, as if on the wind, and in them she heard what he wasn't saying. No one in the world. No one left living, he meant.

Zoey shook her head and tendrils of hair slipped out of the knot and whipped around her face.

Okay. So, however incredible last night had been, one night was what it had to stay. That part was easy.

Forgetting how good it had been…that might be a little harder.

But she had to. For the sake of their friendship.

Dragging herself to her feet, she started back along the beach, towards the jetty where they'd moored the boat the night before. She could already make out a figure standing there, running a hand over the boat. Her heart contracted a little at the sight.

Ash.

Yeah, this might be harder than she'd hoped.

The problem, she mused as she walked, was that Grace had set Ash up as the perfect husband. In her head, Zoey saw the two of them as the ideals of marriage—everything she was looking for. It was only natural, really, that she should fall a little bit in love with him too. Or at least with the idea of him.

That was the part she had to focus on. The *idea* of Ash as part of Ash-and-Grace, couple of the year, was one thing. The *reality* was something different altogether.

Ash the idea was perfect, unattainable, a

dream—and he belonged to Grace. She could admire and adore him from afar, like she might a movie star. That was easy.

Ash the reality was her best friend, broken by the loss of his family, who needed her as a shoulder to cry on, as a support network and as someone to remember Grace with. She could do all that—she had been doing it for two years.

But the first wasn't real. And the second... He didn't need a best friend lusting over him or making things weird just because they got carried away with the romance of being stranded on a desert island, and the adrenaline of running out on yet another wedding. He didn't need a friend idealising him, or imagining him naked all the time.

He just needed her to be his friend. And she could do that.

With a sharp nod to herself, Zoey quickened her step. They'd check out the boat and head back to the hotel—not so she could marry David, but so she could set things right there.

Then she could go home, and she and Ash could go back to being friends again. Just friends.

The only problem with her plan, she realised as she reached the jetty, was that she wasn't entirely sure which of the two Ashes she'd slept with last night.

The ideal or the best friend.

CHAPTER SIX

'HOW'S IT LOOKING?' Zoey's voice called out, closer than he expected, and Ash spun around so fast he clocked his head on the side of the boat. 'Ouch.' She winced. 'Sorry.'

Okay, that was *not* going to help his headache. One he was pretty sure was caused more by stress and confusion and the lack of a pillow than alcohol.

'You surprised me.' Rubbing his temple, he stepped away from the boat and closer to her, eyeing her warily. Which Zoey was this? The carefree one he'd made love to last night, or the frightened one who'd run away from him this morning?

Careful scrutiny revealed neither. This Zoey looked cautious, but not afraid. She also looked determined.

Ash decided not to worry just yet about

what she was determined to *do*. As long as it wasn't marrying David, how bad could it be?

'I'm sorry I ran out on you before.' She bit her bottom lip as she watched him from under her lashes. 'It's sort of a bad habit of mine.'

Ash couldn't help the bark of laughter that escaped from him. 'Well, at least you were wearing a towel instead of a white dress this time.'

Zoey laughed and the sound made his heart feel lighter.

'So? How is the boat looking?'

Okay, so they were avoiding the subject of them for a while. Probably for the best, Ash acknowledged. He wasn't sure he could talk rationally about it until the urge to kiss her again had left his system.

He just wished he knew how long that would take.

It was crazy. He'd never looked at Zoey this way before last night. And now…now it was all he could see.

For distraction, Ash glanced back at the stolen yacht. She wanted to know how it was. He needed to focus on that, and how they were going to get off the island. If that was actually their best move, right now.

'Well, that depends,' he said.

'On what?'

'On what you want to use it for.' He was not above some boat sabotage if it meant keeping her from a wedding he *knew* she didn't really want to go through with. Especially not if her reason for going back was because he'd screwed up and kissed her last night. Not to mention all the other stuff he'd done to her…

Focus on the boat, Ash.

Zoey rolled her eyes. 'I'm not planning on marrying David, if that's what you're worried about.'

'Good.' Relief washed over him. 'Because I was starting to worry about how truly awful last night was for you if your first instinct was to run back to him.'

Colour flooded Zoey's cheeks and Ash started to regret the joke—until she said, almost to herself, '*That* wasn't the problem at all.'

Interesting. Very interesting.

Okay, so not thinking about it and not talking about it wasn't working—in fact, the not thinking part seemed pretty much impossible.

Which meant they needed to deal with it head-on.

Moving closer, Ash couldn't stop himself pressing the point. Male pride, perhaps, he admitted to himself. Or maybe just a desperate need to fix things with his best friend.

'So what was the problem, Zo? Why did you run away from me this morning?'

'I wasn't running away—' she started, then broke off and sighed. 'Okay, fine, I was. I just… I needed to figure some stuff out in my head. Last night was…unexpected.'

'It definitely was,' Ash agreed. He could never have predicted they'd end up here. But now they were, he couldn't imagine how things could be any different. How he could ever get back to looking at Zoey and only seeing a friend.

What had changed the way he saw her? He wasn't even sure. But he had a feeling it had something to do with the way she'd looked at him in that damn cupboard and told him to get her out of there.

Suddenly, it had been the two of them against the world. And that had felt…right.

Zoey was still talking. God, *where* was his focus today?

Still in bed with Zoey Hepburn.

'And I get that we need to talk about it,' Zoey went on as he forced himself to tune back in. This was important. 'So I figure we should probably get that over and done with before we head back to the hotel.'

Over and done with. Well, that was a telling phrase. Ash felt his spirits sink as he realised what she was doing.

She was going to try and brush the whole night under the carpet. Talk about it and then pretend it never happened. And he could understand why, really he could. It wasn't exactly the best timing, or the ideal circumstances. But he knew how not talking about things could fester.

Ash tried to live without regrets these days.

And while he certainly wasn't going to regret making love to Zoey Hepburn—how could he, when it had been the best thing to happen to him in two long years?—Ash knew that if they didn't resolve things properly between them now, he'd regret that later.

He looked back at the boat again. It wasn't in bad shape, considering the battering it had taken in the wind. But he was no expert. It would probably be reckless and irresponsible to try to sail it back now, with the winds still so high, right?

Wiping his hands on the towel he held, he tossed it back into the boat carelessly and smiled. 'Well, then, the good news is we have all the time we need to talk. The boat took a real beating in the storm. Better to wait until I can contact someone to come out and pick us—and it—up safely, I think. Don't you?'

Zoey's eyes went wide at the suggestion and she stammered her way through an agreement. 'Uh, right. Yeah. Sure. I guess.'

'So? Do you want to talk in the villa or shall we take a walk on the beach?' he asked, still smiling easily. He didn't want to spook her any more than necessary.

The way she glanced over at the villa then shook her head told him all he needed to know. She wasn't ready to return to the scene of the crime just yet. Or maybe she was worried about what they'd be tempted to do, alone in there.

He didn't blame her. Just the idea of it had his blood heating and images of her naked in his arms filling his brain.

Ash swallowed. 'Beach it is, then.'

Yeah, the villa was *not* a good idea.

It wasn't that Zoey didn't trust Ash there. She didn't trust herself. Just one kiss from him last night and she'd been clawing his clothes off. Blaming the whisky or the adrenaline or whatever didn't change the truth, now she'd acknowledged it to herself.

She wanted him.

But she couldn't let herself have him.

That way lay a broken heart, for certain.

She'd always been the runner before, but

this time she knew she wouldn't be able to outrun her feelings for Ash if she let herself fall any deeper. He couldn't give her what she craved—a happy marriage, a happily-ever-after. And she couldn't ask him for it either.

He'd given it once, to the person who she'd loved most in the whole world.

It wasn't hers to want.

So she wouldn't.

It had been one night. One stupid night. And that was what it would stay.

Which meant she needed to get them both firmly back on friendship ground again. Quickly.

It would have been easier back in the real world—although there she'd have had her ex-fiancé and both their families to deal with first. So maybe this was for the best.

However tempting it was to just drag him back to the villa…

No. Focus on the friendship.

They strolled back along the beach she'd explored that morning but this time, less pre-occupied with her own thoughts, Zoey noticed more signs of the storm. Palm leaves strewn over the sand, some wood she assumed the builders had been using for the villa had blown out and got stuck in a palm tree. Plants were reduced to sticks, and she could see signs where the waves had crashed far higher than usual, hitting parts of the island usually safe from the sea's ravages.

No wonder the boat wasn't fit to sail.

'So. Are we going to talk?' Ash asked after they'd been walking in awkward silence for a while.

Zoey looked away so he wouldn't see her wince. 'Absolutely. I'll go first.'

'Okay.' Was that amusement she heard in his voice? Well, she was ignoring it. She had a plan here, dammit, and she intended to follow it.

'Right. Well, first off, I think it's really important we agree that this doesn't affect our friendship,' she said, in what she thought was a reasonable tone.

'And you have an idea for how we can do that?' Ash guessed.

Zoey nodded. 'Absolutely. What happened on this island *stays* on this island. As far as the rest of the world is concerned—hell, as far as *we're* concerned once we get off here—it never happened. Okay?'

He didn't answer. Zoey walked a few more steps before she realised he wasn't with her either.

She turned to face him, her bare feet sinking into the sand. She should have known he'd make this difficult.

'What?' She placed her hands on her hips and tried not to scowl.

'You're beautiful when you scowl, you know.' He was smiling. Why was he smiling?

'I'm not scowling. And did you not hear me on the forgetting all about it part?'

'I heard.' He stepped closer. 'In fact, I heard you say—very clearly—that we had to forget this *once we get off the island.*'

Zoey swallowed. Hard. 'What are you saying?'

Ash's smile was almost wolfish. 'We're still on the island, Zo.'

She looked around her. Sea. Sand. Sun. No one else for miles and miles of water...

'So we are,' she said faintly.

Another step and he was right before her, his hands coming to rest on her hips. 'Look, I'm not saying you're wrong. Our timing sucks, and you have a million things to sort out when we get back to the real world. And your friendship is worth more to me than anything else.'

'But?' There was always a but. She could tell from the heat in his eyes he wasn't *actually* agreeing with her.

Hell, she wasn't sure even *she* agreed with herself right now.

'But all I can think of right now is stripping that lovely pink dress from your skin again.'

A shiver went through her at his words, and Ash chuckled. 'You thinking about it too?' he asked.

Words were beyond her, so she just nodded.

There was no alcohol this time. No runaway adrenaline still coursing through their veins. No excuses left between them. If they did this again it was on them. Their choice, their want.

And oh, she wanted.

Besides, she reasoned in her lust-addled mind, if this was all she could ever have of Ash Carmichael—this strange stolen time away from real world—shouldn't she make the most of it?

Later she'd get back to reality. To worrying about where she was going to live and what she was going to do about David, and how to repair her and Ash's friendship after they fractured it once more.

But right now…

Zoey stopped thinking, stretched up on her tiptoes and kissed her best friend.

His heart was still racing. He had sand in places sand should never go, he was covered in sweat, his bare skin was probably burning in the sun and he couldn't bring himself to care. Because Zoey was draped over him, naked and more relaxed than he'd ever seen her in his life.

And this time they'd been sober. This time he had no doubts at all about her state of mind or whether this was a good idea.

It was an *excellent* idea. They should definitely do it more often.

Quite how that would work out with Zoey's 'we should focus on our friendship' plan he wasn't sure, but he figured he had time. He wasn't going anywhere, after all—and she wasn't wrong. Their friendship *was* the most important thing.

But if, once they'd got back to the real world and Zoey had set things straight with David and moved on properly, they decided to try this again, in an actual bed next time…would that really be such a bad thing?

He didn't think so. And he hoped that, over time, Zoey might come to think the same way.

He just had to be patient.

Ash ran a hand down Zoey's naked side and cursed the fact that patience wasn't one of his many virtues. But he could do it. If it meant he got to have Zoey this way again.

'You okay?' he asked softly.

'Mmm,' she responded, rubbing her cheek against his bare chest.

See? That was a good start, right?

'So, do you still want to talk some more?' Personally, he had some much better ideas for how they could spend their time on the island, but if she needed to talk to feel comfortable with things between them then he'd talk.

But Zoey shook her head, her dark, tangled hair tickling his chin. 'What else is there to say? The minute we get off this island, this is over and we go back to being just friends. Right?'

A chill settled over him, despite the sunshine. 'If that's what you want.'

Zoey pushed herself up against his chest, leaning over him and frowning. 'It's what needs to happen.'

'So you said.' Ash shielded his eyes from the sun as he took in her expression. 'Remind me why that is again?'

'Because…because we're friends. And that's all.'

There was something behind her eyes. Something he couldn't quite interpret. But, whatever it was, it was holding her back.

Ash sat up, pulling her with him so she sat curled up against him. 'What's the matter, Zoey? Is it David? Or…' Grace. It must be Grace.

Of course this was weird—for him as well as her. But he'd lived without his wife for two years now, and he knew that she'd want him to find happiness wherever he could.

But for Zoey… Grace had been more family to her than her own parents. Closer than a sibling even, for a lonely only child. It stood to reason that she'd feel she was betraying her friend, even now Grace was gone.

Well, hopefully, that was something she'd come to terms with in time.

Time. Time passed, whatever he chose to do with it.

For two years he'd never even imagined himself with another woman, despite the blind dates people tried to arrange, or the obvious set up dinner parties his mother kept throwing whenever he was in London.

Now…now it was hard to imagine *not* being with Zoey again, not having her in his life, his bed.

Maybe it was because she'd always been there. A constant part of his life. Familiar and comfortable and easy. And okay, maybe the last twenty-four hours had seen their relationship take on a different aspect, but in some ways it felt perfectly natural.

Ash had no illusions about for ever or true love—like he'd told Zoey, he'd already found that once and didn't expect to again. But a friendship that also had passion, the way his and Zoey's did, that was something more than he'd ever imagined having again.

Quite honestly, now he'd had her in his arms this way, it was hard to imagine letting her go.

But Zoey was already pulling away.

'It's not David. Or anything else, really. I just think that we'd be better off as friends. Like I said, your friendship is too important to me to risk it on a fling.'

A fling. Was that what this was? Probably, he supposed. It wasn't as if he was lining up to be the next groom Zoey ran away from, anyway. He just wanted to enjoy what they had right now.

Ash didn't spend much time thinking about the future. He'd learned the hard way how easily it could be ripped away from him. He wasn't imagining for ever or happily-ever-after.

He just knew he didn't want this to end yet.

But was that just his libido talking? Quite possibly.

And Zoey was right. They couldn't risk their friendship. It was all either of them had, some days.

'If that's how you feel,' he said neutrally. Because, to be honest, he wasn't entirely sure how *he* felt. So maybe they'd better go with her instincts.

'It is,' she said firmly.

Except Zoey's instincts were notoriously awful. Could he really rely on them for something as important as this?

'Just…promise me we'll keep talking,' he said, looking up at her as she stood, gloriously naked in the sunshine on the deserted beach. 'That you won't shut me out or start avoiding me now. That you'll always be honest with me about how you're feeling.'

She needed to be able to talk to someone and he was it. Which meant they couldn't let a little sex make things difficult between them now.

'Absolutely,' Zoey said with a firm nod.

'Good.' Plus, as long as they kept talking, stayed close, it would give them a chance to figure this out.

Whatever was between them, Ash had a feeling it wouldn't be put back in its box as easily as Zoey seemed to think it would.

He just wished he could shake the feeling that she was keeping something from him. That her reasons for calling things off weren't as simple as she was making out. They made sense, of course, whether he fully agreed with them or not.

Still, he was certain there was something else.

'Zo?' he asked softly. She bit her lip as she

looked down at him. 'Is there something else? Anything else that's bothering you. That you're worried about?'

Her lips parted just a fraction, as if she were about to say something. Then her gaze darted away from him and out towards the ocean beyond, her eyes widening.

'Look! A boat!' Bounding over him in a move that caused her body to sway in a way that made Ash catch his breath, Zoey waved her hot pink dress over her head at the sailors. Ash reached for his trousers and pulled them on, less comfortable with his own nudity than Zoey apparently was.

Or perhaps she's just so desperate to get away from me, from this conversation, that she doesn't care about being naked in front of strangers.

He shook the thought away. Why would she be running from him?

Except she was. Tugging her dress over her head as she ran, Zoey raced towards the boat—a rescue service from one of the local hotels, by the look of things—laughing and calling out to their rescuers.

Apparently, their escape to paradise together was over.

CHAPTER SEVEN

IT WASN'T UNTIL she was safely on the boat that Zoey considered what she was heading back to.

Until then she'd been far too busy remembering what she was leaving behind.

Ash was quiet on the journey, and she knew the question she hadn't answered had to be weighing as heavily on him as it was on her. But how was she supposed to say, *I'm terrified that if I spend any longer with you this way I'll fall so deeply in love I can't get out again*?

He didn't want for ever—he'd had that. She knew that Ash made a point of living in the moment these days—even if it drove his father, and shareholders, crazy when it came to the business. He'd already had what she was still searching for.

And she had to believe that one day, against all the odds, she'd find it.

Then maybe she could make it through an actual wedding of her own.

'Want me to come with you to talk to David?' Ash asked quietly from beside her as the stood at the rail and watched the hotel grow closer and closer.

Zoey shook her head. 'I think I'd better do this one alone.' She looked down at herself. 'Hopefully after a shower and a change of clothes.'

The boat docked and two men jumped over the rail to tie it up. Ash helped her step over onto the jetty, just like he had the night before, in the middle of the storm. How different things were now, though.

Since last night *everything* felt different. Most of all Zoey herself.

'Where the hell have you been?'

Zoey winced at the voice. She'd been expecting David, but no. First on the scene were her parents. Just perfect.

Her father's face was bright red as he stalked

down the jetty towards them. Part sunburn, part fury, Zoey decided dispassionately.

'We didn't fly all the way out here just so you could run off with some other bloke the night before your wedding!' He waved a hand vaguely at Ash, who sensibly put his hands in his pockets and looked away.

No, you came here for the free bar and the chance to cosy up to potential clients, Zoey thought, but didn't say.

'I'm sorry, Dad. I couldn't go through with it. Ash— You remember Ash, right? Grace's husband?' Her father looked blankly at him. Zoey wasn't all that surprised. It wasn't as if she'd spent a lot of time socialising with her parents and friends together, or filling her mum and dad in on the events of her life.

They were far more preoccupied with their own lives and dramas, anyway.

'You ran off with your *best friend's husband?'* her mother shrieked, because clearly this whole situation wasn't embarrassing enough as it was.

'Widower,' Ash corrected calmly. 'And all I did was help Zoey find some time and space to decide what she wanted to do next.' Which wasn't *entirely* true, unless Ash counted fantastic sex as some sort of decision matrix.

Which it might have been, really. There was no way Zoey could go back to the same old boring sex she'd had with David after one night with Ash.

Her parents weren't listening to him, though. Or to her, really. They'd turned the whole event into the Hugh and Tanya show, as usual.

'I always knew you were just like your father,' her mother, Tanya, said, looking accusingly at her husband.

'Oh, really?' Hugh replied, his tone sharp. 'Because I was just thinking she was just like her mother. Which one of us was it that ran off with the waiter at our anniversary dinner?'

'And who had a three-year affair with my best friend?' Tanya shot back.

'You know, I can't help but think sometimes

the world would be a better place if one of *you* hadn't shown up at the church on your wedding day,' Zoey said, safe in the knowledge that neither of them were listening to her. They were too busy throwing past misdeeds in each other's faces.

They'd make up later, Zoey knew from bitter past experience. They'd be all over each other in the bar for at least an hour or two before something else set them at each other's throats.

'Except if they hadn't married you'd have never been born,' Ash pointed out. At least someone listened to her.

Then Zoey caught sight of David, pale and with huge circles under his eyes, approaching them on the jetty.

'Even so,' Zoey murmured, 'it might have been for the best.'

Ash watched, helpless, as David led Zoey away, back towards the hotel.

Their wedding venue, if she'd stayed. Was

he taking her back to the bridal suite right now? What would he do? Say?

Ash knew he had absolutely no right in the world to feel jealous, but that didn't seem to be stopping him.

Zoey couldn't go back to him, could she? Not because of last night, or what they'd shared. But because he wanted her to be happy—and he was more sure than ever now that David couldn't give her that.

Mr and Mrs Hepburn were still at each other's throats, filling the air with accusations and curses that Ash didn't care to hear. Leaving them behind, he headed towards the hotel, hoping a hot shower would help wash away some of the emotions last night had raised.

'You.' The word—spat at him with real venom—gave him pause.

With a small sigh, he turned to the speaker. 'Benji. Hi.' David's best man was a small rat of a guy who seemed to want to compensate for his lack of size with sheer volume and theatrics. Not unlike Zoey's parents, Ash decided, hiding a lack of love with an excess of showy passion.

'David always said that you were trouble. That you had a thing for Zoey.' Benji was trying to get up in his space—at least that was what Ash thought he was doing. Being a full head shorter than him meant that Benji had to maintain some distance just to be able to look him in the eye.

Ash thought about crouching down to make things easier for him, but figured that would just be patronising. Tempting though it was.

'Look, Benji, whatever you think was going on here…' Ash trailed off. How could he truly complete that sentence without lying horribly? Sure, maybe his intentions in taking Zoey away from the island had been entirely honourable, but that didn't change what had actually happened next.

'I think you wanted Zoey for yourself, so you stole her away when she was vulnerable. David says you never liked him, never thought he was good enough for Zoey—as if *she* wasn't the one with the track record for destroying lives!'

'Hey,' Ash snapped. 'That's enough. Zoey made a decision—I just helped her out.'

'I'm sure you did,' Benji said, with enough sleaze in his voice to make Ash feel even dirtier than he already did.

Suddenly, the full implications of their actions seemed to settle on his shoulders and he felt older, more tired and more disgusted with himself than he'd been in years.

Whatever his intentions, he'd made things harder for Zoey. He should have just insisted she *talk* to David, like any normal person would if they were having doubts the night before their wedding. Like Grace would have persuaded her to do.

Why hadn't he? Was Benji right? Had he wanted Zoey for himself?

He'd never really thought about Zoey that way until yesterday. She was Grace's friend, so would have been completely off-limits even if he *hadn't* been totally in love with his wife. But when Grace was alive he'd never looked beyond her—he hadn't needed or wanted to. She'd been his world.

And since his world had come crashing down around him, romance had honestly been the last thing on his mind. Even if it hadn't, he doubted he would have even considered Zoey a possibility.

She was his friend. His best friend. Possibly his only friend.

It had taken some pretty extreme circumstances to get him to see beyond that. To look at her in the light of the storm and really see her—wild and free and stubborn and so, so beautiful. Someone who trusted him to help her, who could laugh with him even when everything was falling apart.

And now? What was she now?

Still his friend, he hoped.

And she was right. They had to forget everything that had happened on the island.

Because back here in the real world, with David waiting on the dock, Ash could see at last the answer Zoey hadn't given him on the island—the real reason they couldn't carry this on.

She wanted a happily-ever-after marriage—she wanted for ever. And he'd already given his away with his heart.

He loved Zoey, of course he did. She was family, practically. And he wanted her—that much was obvious after last night.

But neither of those things added up to what Zoey wanted from her future. Not to mention that he had no idea if she'd even *want* him to feature in that future.

He had to let her go so she could find the true love she was looking for. However much his selfish heart wanted to keep her for himself.

They hadn't talked about the repercussions of their actions before they took them. If they had, they'd probably never have even kissed. Overthinking things was a definite passion-killer.

Except…oh, God. There was definitely one thing that they *should* have talked about before sleeping together. Ash hadn't thought beyond making sure that Zoey was happy with what they were doing.

He hadn't thought about protection at all, too overcome with lust to remember even that basic necessity.

Probably because he hadn't needed to, for years. Two years of celibacy had been preceded by Grace being pregnant or them trying. And even before that Grace had been on the Pill, and they'd both been tested and clean. He hadn't thought about contraceptives since he was a *teenager.*

And he couldn't think about them right now. He had to focus on getting Zoey through the next twenty-four hours first.

Most of all, she needed to get through this latest wedding breakdown with her sanity intact, and without ruining her reputation more than ever. A runaway bride was one thing. A cheating runaway bride was another. Plus, there were the practicalities to consider—she was living with David, had given up her flat last year. So where was she planning on going?

'Look, Benji. Here's the full story, okay? Zoey had cold feet. She wanted to get away from here to think, so I took her out on the boat. A storm came up so we sheltered in a half-renovated villa my company owns. It was dusty, dirty and the least romantic place you can imagine.' And yet... 'This morning we waited for a rescue boat as ours had been damaged in the storm. Then we came back so that Zoey could talk to David. It was as simple and as boring as that. Okay?'

All true—except for the major omissions. But Benji had no right to that information anyway, so Ash didn't feel too guilty about keeping it from him.

'That's really all?' Benji asked, his tone both doubtful and disappointed.

Ash gave a sharp nod. 'Now, if you don't mind, I am in desperate need of a shower.'

He brushed past the best man, heading for his room and hoping that hot water could wash away memories.

And guilt.

* * *

This. This was the part she hated the most. Explaining herself. Justifying her unjustifiable actions.

'David…'

'No.' David cut her off as he jabbed at the button, waiting for the lift that would take them all the way to the honeymoon suite on the top floor.

Zoey looked down at her ruined pink dress and thought about the beautiful ivory lace one that was hanging from the wardrobe in the suite. The dress she'd never wear now. Just like all the others.

They rode the lift in silence. Zoey stared straight ahead, avoiding catching her own eye in any of the reflections glinting from the mirror-lined walls. She didn't want to see the guilt there.

Finally, after what seemed like an eternity, the lift doors opened onto the top corridor and David strode out towards the honeymoon suite door. Zoey followed, her steps more hesitant.

She wished she'd spent more of the time since she'd left on that boat preparing for this conversation. But instead she'd found herself debating and stressing over an entirely different problem. One she couldn't even have predicted having twenty-four hours earlier.

But at least her night with Ash had made one thing very, very clear: there was no way she could marry David now.

Even if she confessed all and he still wanted her, she knew it wouldn't be fair—to either of them. She might not be able to find a future with Ash, but she was damned if she was going to settle for anything less than she'd felt with him last night.

How depressing was it that her most fulfilling relationship might actually be a one-night stand?

She stepped into the bridal suite and the door swung shut behind her, closing with an almost inaudible click. No slammed doors, no drama.

Except that David looked like he might explode any second now. Even standing with his back to her, staring out of the window at the blue, blue sea that surrounded them, Zoey could read the tension and the anger in his shoulders, his arms, even his legs.

David was furious. Understandably.

'I'm sorry,' she said quickly. It was best to get that one out immediately, although she was under no illusion that it was the last time she'd be saying it in this conversation.

'Do you ever wonder what it says about you that you have to say that so often?' David spun around from the window, his handsome face ugly with hatred.

Zoey recoiled. David had always been an attractive man in a bland, easy way. No sharp features, just neat hair, neat jaw line, regularly spaced eyes and so on. Like a stock image, or one of those photos that came in a picture frame when you bought it.

He looked ordinary, in an attractive way.

But not now.

'I shouldn't have run. I should have talked to you first. I'm sorry,' she repeated, trying to keep her tone calm and conciliatory, even though her heart was racing.

'What you should have done was go through with the damned wedding!' he yelled, slamming his hand down on the desk at the window.

Zoey flinched at the crack of his palm against the wood. 'I'm sorry. I got cold feet. I just… I don't think we would have made each other happy for the rest of our lives.'

'So? Marriage isn't about being *happy,* Zoey. You've always had some sort of idealised view of what a relationship should be, but it's not all roses and sunshine all the time. Nobody has that!'

'I know. I don't want perfect,' she said softly. 'I just want perfect *for me.*'

'And I'm not, is that it?' David shook his head, his face red with anger as he stalked forward towards her. 'You *cannot* truly be trying to tell me this is *my fault.*' The last two words came out as a yell, and Zoey shrank back against the door.

'No, no. That's not what I'm saying.'

But David was past listening. He took another slow, deliberate step forward and Zoey found her hands moving instinctively in front of her as if to ward him off.

Calm down, Zo, she told herself, trying to keep her breathing even. *It's just David. Nothing to be scared of.*

Except she was.

'Do you know, there's an actual support group.' David's voice was low and dangerous. 'For your exes. For all the men you've tried to destroy with your cheating, lying ways.'

Zoey swallowed. She wanted to deny the cheating accusation but, after last night, how could she?

'I… No. I didn't know that.'

'Oh, yes.' Another step closer. 'They reached out to me after I proposed to you. As soon as they heard you'd said yes. They keep tabs on you, you see.'

'They're spying on me?' Because that was creepy as all get-out. How many of them were there? Did they meet up for coffee or something, just to talk about how awful she was?

Zoey wanted to ask more questions but she suspected this wasn't quite the time.

Still. The idea of a support group for men she'd dumped at the altar, or just before, was frankly terrifying.

What sort of an awful person was she, anyway?

'They said they wanted to try and save other poor fools from their fate.' David's mouth twisted up in a sneer. 'Of course, I told them this time was different. That *I* was different.'

'I wasn't planning on running out on you,' Zoey said miserably.

David scoffed. 'Oh, of course not. What was it you told me on our third date? When we talked about past relationships?' He put one finger to his jaw as if trying to remember. 'That's right. You told me that all those other men hadn't been right for you—and you weren't right for them either. Funny how you were the only one to realise that—and not until you'd dragged them all the way to the altar with you. Tell me honestly, Zoey. Do you get a kick out of destroying men's lives?'

'No!' Zoey's eyes widened as his words hit home. 'No, David, you've got it wrong. I didn't… I never meant to hurt you. Any of you. I just… I couldn't go through with it. It's me, not—'

'Don't say it,' David snapped. 'I know this isn't *my* fault. What I don't understand is how you think you can keep doing this to people.'

'Would it have been better to marry you knowing we'd both be unhappy?' she asked softly.

'Yes! Of course it would!'

Zoey blinked. 'I don't… I don't understand.'

'Because you're just thinking about *you*.' David spat the words out, his eyes filled with hatred where she'd seen love only days before. How could she have got this so wrong?

'So explain it to me,' she said.

'Every marriage has, at best, a fifty-fifty shot, right?' David said.

'I guess.' Of course, she suspected it was rather less if the bride ran away and slept with another man the night before.

'So why not just give it a go? Would it have

killed you to have just *shown up* for once? To *not* run when your stupid instincts told you to? To go through with what you promised for *my* sake?' His hands moved as he spoke, growing more animated as he explained. He had to have been thinking about this all night, Zoey realised.

'You would have wanted me to marry you even if I was having doubts?' *Serious* doubts. 'Why?'

'Because at least then I wouldn't be the laughing stock of my company, my family and all our friends!' David yelled and the words echoed off the walls, making Zoey's ears ring.

'I'm sorry if you feel embarrassed...' she started, but David wasn't done talking yet.

'Do you even realise how much was riding on this marriage? Why do you think I went to such lengths to make sure it happened? It wasn't just for my sake—it was for the sake of the company. Mine and your parents', for that matter. We had *plans, Zoey.*'

'Wait.' Zoey frowned, trying to make sense

of his words. 'You wanted to marry me because of Mum and Dad's *company*? I was a business deal?'

David waved a hand to dismiss her incredulity. 'Not only for that, of course. It was just convenient that our industries lined up nicely. The company needs a boost right now and your parents are hoping to take early retirement, so I could have taken it over and built it up ready for when my own father retires, and I become CEO of the whole empire.'

'Not *only* for that,' she repeated faintly. Then she felt the anger rising, her instincts screaming that they'd been right all along. 'Was anything about this relationship actually about me?'

David rolled his eyes. 'Of course it was. I wouldn't have proposed if you weren't beautiful, and good company—in bed and out.'

'Or if you weren't in love with me,' Zoey pressed, but David didn't even dignify that one with an answer. Zoey's guilt started ebbing away, like water down a storm drain.

'And, to be honest, the fact that you were a

challenge—that other people said you wouldn't go through with it—that only made me keener.'

Zoey tried to get her head around all the new information swirling around her brain. Tried to reconcile the man in front of her with the one she'd said yes to when he got down on one knee.

It seemed impossible.

'So what you're saying is that you wanted me to marry you, even if it would make me unhappy, just so you could do a business deal, show me off and brag about bagging the runaway bride?'

'What else do you think marriage *is,* Zoey?' David asked, sounding astonished at her naivety. 'It's deals and trophies. Marriage is the ultimate status symbol. You have to marry someone who enhances your own position.' He waved a hand in her direction. 'You might not have much social standing or money yourself, and your job barely qualifies as a career, but your parents' company makes up for that. Add in the fact that you're beautiful and charming, and suddenly you're of interest to people. But most of all you were a challenge. If I married you, people would know that I must have something other men didn't.'

Zoey sank back against the door as if she'd been punched in the stomach. '*That* was why you wanted to marry me?'

'Of course it was.' David's mouth twisted into a cruel, mocking smile. 'Oh, Zoey. You didn't *really* think it was *love*, did you? Nobody believes in that these days.'

I do, Zoey thought.

She knew that love was real—she'd seen it. And maybe she hadn't been lucky enough to find it for herself yet, but that didn't mean she had to settle for anything less.

And *definitely* not being a sign of manliness or a business deal for a guy like David.

Twisting her engagement ring off her right ring finger, Zoey held it out to David, who snatched it from her.

'I'm sorry this didn't work out,' she said softly. 'I'll pack up my stuff and get out of your way.'

'You do that. I'll stay on here for the next

couple of weeks, like we planned. Give you time to get out of the London flat too.'

Pushing past her, David left the room and Zoey was alone for the first time since the desert island.

She took advantage of the solitude to crumple to the floor and sob.

CHAPTER EIGHT

ZOEY LET HERSELF cry until the tears stung her sore eyes and her chest hurt from wrenching sobs. If Grace had been there, she knew her best friend would have rubbed her back, handed her tissues, whispered encouragement and told her to *let it all out.*

So she did.

And then, when it was all out there, a mess of a life in tears and snot and misery, she picked herself up, washed her face and forced herself to face reality.

Grace wasn't there any longer to help her when she screwed up. To ask the important, searching questions that always led Zoey to her best path forward. Of course, if Grace had been there, Zoey wouldn't be in half the mess she was. Grace would have spotted what David was truly after long before Zoey had.

And if Grace was alive there was no way she'd have slept with Ash in the first place.

Still. Without her best friend on hand, Zoey would just have to do the asking *and* the answering.

'What do I want to happen next?' she asked herself aloud. 'I want… I want to go home. That's easy.' Except she didn't *have* a home any more. She'd been living in David's flat for months. So, back to her parents' house it was.

If they'd still have her.

'Worst case scenario, I find a hotel or something for a few nights until I can find somewhere—anywhere—to rent.' She'd picked herself up from nothing before, she could do it again. As soon as she was back in the right country, anyway.

'Okay, next question. What do I need to do to make that happen?' She could ask Ash to help her change her plane ticket home for a flight today. He could probably help her with a transfer off the island and to the airport on the mainland too, given his connections at the hotel and in the travel industry generally.

She already had her passport and ticket in her hand when reality hit, and she sank down to sit on the bed.

Yes, Ash would help her. He'd do whatever it took to get her home safely, she knew that. And he'd do it as a friend.

Except…that wasn't really all he was any more, however much she was trying to pretend otherwise. Sex changed things, whether they wanted it to or not. It was going to take some time to get them back to where they'd been before—if they ever managed it.

But that wasn't the worst part. The worst part was that it would be so, so easy *not* to go back to being friends.

So easy to let Ash travel back to London with her, if he wanted. To suggest she stay the night in his spare room, in that awful sparse flat he barely even lived in, only for them to end up in his bed together, recreating their finest desert island moments.

And from there it would be a short step into friends with benefits territory. She'd be a mate and a warm body in bed whenever he was in town. And she'd never ask him for anything more, because she already knew he couldn't give it.

It was good that Ash was getting back out into the world again, moving forward after Grace's death. But it couldn't be with her. Because she wanted so much more than that out of life.

Zoey knew—after one night or ten years, depending on how she looked at it—that it would be too damn easy to fall in love with Ash Carmichael. And it would break her heart when he couldn't love her back.

Which meant, for now, she had to do it without Ash. She had to take charge of her own life and move forward without him, without Grace, without her parents, without David or any other members of the Zoey's Exes Support Group.

Just Zoey.

Suddenly, the weight on her shoulders started to lessen, just a little. And the tears in her eyes were all dried up.

Maybe that was the key.

Maybe it was time to stop running away from her life, from her mistakes, and start facing them head-on instead.

She still wasn't entirely sure what she was going to do when she got back to London. But she knew she would be doing it alone. For herself, by herself.

Ash was just finishing packing his case when Zoey knocked on the hotel room door.

'How's David?' he asked as he stood aside to let her in. He scanned her face, taking in the red-rimmed eyes and dark circles, the pinched expression that made her look less like his Zoey, somehow. Less vibrant. Less alive.

He wanted to wrap her up in his arms and ask how *she* was, how he could make it better. And another, less civilised part of him really wanted to find David and hit him for making her look like that.

Except he knew that David wasn't the wrongdoer in this situation. He and Zoey were.

At least, that was what he thought until

Zoey sat on the edge of his bed and filled him in on their conversation.

'Wait. He wanted to marry you for a *business deal?*'

'Oh, not just that,' Zoey replied airily. 'He had worse reasons, don't forget.'

'To prove he could get what other guys couldn't? To show you off as some sort of trophy?'

Zoey shrugged, her slim shoulders rising then slumping back down. 'Apparently my talent for screwing up weddings and relationships is legendary.'

'At least it is now David's been telling everyone your personal history so he can brag about overcoming it,' Ash muttered, the urge to punch rising in him again.

'Yeah. I dread to think what stories he's going to tell about me now.' She sighed. 'I can't see me getting asked out on a date again for a while.'

'Good,' Ash said without thinking. Zoey shot him a look and he groped for an explanation. 'I mean, maybe it's for the best. You can spend some time alone, figure out what you want, before you get back out there.' That sounded better than, *Now I've seen you naked I'm going to be insanely and irrationally jealous of anyone else who ever gets the opportunity, up to and including your doctor*, right?

'Right.' Zoey looked away as she answered and Ash forced himself to remember that she *knew* what she wanted. She just couldn't ever seem to find it.

And David was, most definitely, not the man for her.

Could *he* be?

The thought brushed through his mind like the sea breeze, stopping Ash halfway through the motion of folding a T-shirt.

It was tempting, he had to admit. The idea of letting Zoey into his life as more than a friend. Of being what she needed.

Except he couldn't.

She wanted true love, and he'd already given his heart away. Apparently death had a no returns policy.

He was too sad, too broken for Zoey's exuberant search for love.

As long as there were no consequences to their night together...

He needed to talk to her about it. But how was he supposed to bring it up?

Hey, Zo, you know I'm an idiot who hasn't had sex in two years and really only with my dead wife before that? Totally forgot about the existence of contraceptives as a thing. Appreciate that's totally on me but still... Kind of hoping it's one of those things you have covered...?

Given that he was dealing with a woman whose back-up plan to escape a wedding was climbing out of a window that was far too small for her, he wasn't sure what the odds were on that one.

Still. They definitely had to talk.

'What are your plans now?' he asked awkwardly.

'For dating?' Zoey asked, looking confused.

Right. He'd moved on mentally from their previous conversation, but not verbally. 'No.

Well, yes, if you want to talk about that. But I meant more...now you're not getting married today. You're supposed to be having your honeymoon here, right? So, are you going to stay?'

Zoey shook her head so hard that her hair whipped round and caught him in the face as he sat down beside her on the bed. 'Definitely not. David will, apparently—he's paid for it, after all. So it's probably best if I was somewhere else. You know, like the other side of the world. At least until he's calmed down a bit. Besides, it'll give me a chance to clear out my stuff from his flat.'

'Where are you going to stay?' Ash wanted to offer her his spare room, but he wasn't sure she'd accept. And maybe she was right. Maybe they did need some distance between them for a little while.

'With my parents.' She said it like someone else might say, *In hell*, and Ash decided distance was overrated anyway.

'You could have my spare room.'

She gave him a small sad smile. 'Thanks.

But I'll try Mum and Dad's first, at least. If they're still talking to me by the time they get home. It shouldn't take me long to find a new flat anyway.'

It all felt wrong to Ash. 'Want me to sort a flight home to London for you at least?' What was the point of being heir to a luxury travel business if you couldn't fix something like this for a friend?

But Zoey shook her head again, less violently this time. 'I appreciate the offer, but I'll sort it. This is my screw-up. I need to fix it myself.'

Ash frowned. 'Hey, you didn't screw up.'

She flashed him a disbelieving look. 'I really did, Ash.'

'You made the right decision for you and your future happiness,' Ash corrected her. 'Your timing might suck, but you still did the right thing in the end.'

'I know,' Zoey replied. 'I mean, I knew it for sure when David told me all the reasons I should have gone through with the wedding anyway. He was the wrong man for me.'

'I'd argue he's the wrong man for anybody,' Ash said. 'But yeah, you're definitely better off without him.'

'Which is why I'm going to go and find someone to take me to the airport and get on the next plane back to London that my credit card can stand.'

'You're sure you won't let me sort it for you?' He couldn't fix anything else in her world, but this one he could. If she'd let him.

'Thank you, but no.' She sighed as she got to her feet. 'You know, I realised something. My whole life I've been looking for someone else to fix my life for me. Grace would take me in so I could escape my parents rowing. Then the two of you would support me every time I screwed up another relationship— relationships I was only in because I was looking for some man to give me my happily-ever-after. Hell, I even needed you to help me escape my own wedding. Not just to get me off the island, but to prove to myself I was right to leave by—' She broke off, her cheeks pink, and Ash knew *exactly* what she wasn't saying.

By screwing you instead. Was that all he'd been? A way to be sure that she didn't want to be with David?

It hadn't felt like that to him.

'Anyway, the point is, maybe you're right. Maybe it is good I won't be able to find anyone willing to date me within a hundred-mile radius of David. Because...' She took a deep breath before continuing. 'Because it's time to stop looking for that happily-ever-after as if it'll fix my problems. It's time to make my life what I want it to be on my own, for a change.'

Ash swallowed. It wasn't that he didn't want Zoey to take hold of the reins of her own life. He did. So why did he feel as if he was being cast aside too?

'That's good. Really, Zo. Just...everyone needs a friend sometimes too, right?' he said. 'So don't forget. You don't have to do it all on your own. I'm here for you, if you need me.'

The smile she gave him was so soft and loving it made his chest ache. 'I know. You're my best friend, Ash. You're all I have left now. Which is why…'

'That's all we can ever be,' Ash finished, so she didn't have to. 'I get that. And I get you wanting to make it by yourself. But—'

She groaned. 'Does there have to be a but?'

'Hopefully not.' Ash tried to find a delicate way to put what he had to say, and failed. 'Look, I'm totally on board with the pretending last night never happened and going back to being friends.' Well, not *totally,* since that meant never seeing her naked again. But he could work with it, for her sake. 'But I have to say something.'

'What, Ash?' She tilted her head to the side as she looked at him, as if she were waiting for some poetic or romantic pronouncement.

Boy, was she going to be disappointed.

'We didn't… We were reckless. I didn't use protection. Did you…?'

He knew her answer before she spoke. The colour drained from her cheeks, leaving her eyes huge in her face.

'David and I were doing this stupid abstinence thing for six weeks before the wedding. Plus he said he wanted to try for a honeymoon baby. So I went off the Pill two months ago.' Her words were a whisper.

Something seemed to freeze inside him at her answer. *There could be a baby.*

And of course Zoey wouldn't want that, just when she was taking control of her life again. But part of him couldn't help but imagine a whole new future for them, in that brief second before Zoey started talking again.

'I'm sure… I mean, the chances have to be low. What with all the stress and so on. I think that makes this sort of thing more difficult, right?' She looked up at him, chewing on her lower lip, and he realised that *he* was the voice of experience in this matter.

'Uh, yeah. I think so.' In truth, he could barely remember. After all, he and Grace had been focusing on trying to *get* pregnant, not hoping it wouldn't happen.

God, this was such a mess.

'Right. So, probably nothing to worry about.'

The frown line between her eyes said she was worrying anyway, though.

'Probably not,' Ash said, in what he hoped was a reassuring manner. She was right. Grace had spent months planning to get pregnant—working out optimal times and strategies, adjusting their diets and habits, reading everything she could get her hands on about maximising fertility. There had been thermometers every morning to check when she was ovulating, calls for lunchtime quickies on optimal days—and still it had taken them nine months to get pregnant.

The chances that he and Zoey had conceived in one accidental hook-up—okay, two—had to be low. Surely.

'But...you'll let me know?' he asked, looking into her worried eyes. 'If there's, well, anything to know.'

'Of course,' she replied quickly. 'Of course I will. But right now I'd better get to the airport.'

'Can I take you?' Suddenly, he didn't want to let her out of his sight.

She shook her head. 'I'll get the hotel reception to help me. I'm hoping I can trade in my transfer and flight home from two weeks from now to today.'

'If you need any help, or anything...'

'I'll phone,' Zoey said. But he knew from the too-quick smile she threw him that she wouldn't. 'Give me a call next time you're in London for more than a night, yeah?'

'I will. We can...get dinner or something.'

'Sounds good.' Her smile grew strained. 'Bye, Ash.'

'Bye.'

And then she was gone. And Ash felt suddenly very, very alone again.

Pregnant.

The word echoed around Zoey's head the whole way to the airport.

She heard it in the waves around the speedboat that took her from the hotel island to the mainland, and in the rumble of tyres on the road of the minibus that took her to the terminal. It was in the roar of the planes taking off and landing.

'Pregnant?' the girl behind the counter at the drinks stall in the airport said. Zoey blinked until the girl repeated what she'd *actually* said. 'Coffee?'

Wasn't caffeine bad for the baby?

No. Because there was no baby. Even she wasn't that unlucky, right?

'Black,' she said. 'And strong, please.'

Sitting cradling her cup of coffee, she tried to think through all the events of the last thirty-six hours without her head exploding.

It wasn't easy.

But what it came down to was just what she'd told Ash. It was time to stop waiting around for someone to save her, love her, marry her, give her the family life she craved. Instead, she needed to fight for and carve out a life she could love for herself.

However hard that was.

That was why she hadn't let Ash help her get home—or even see her off the island. She knew that if he'd come with her to the airport it would have been far too easy to start relying on him again. Even if she managed to avoid slipping into the casual relationship with him that she'd foreseen when she'd started planning her return trip, just needing someone else to save her rankled now.

She needed to go it alone. It was past time.

Which didn't mean she wasn't already missing him like crazy.

Zoey took another sip of coffee to stifle a groan. What had she been thinking? She'd screwed up in the past before, but never quite like this. Never 'run out on a wedding thousands of miles from home, got shipwrecked and had unprotected sex with my best friend' screwed up. This was a whole new level of Zoey catastrophe.

No wonder her parents drank so much.

She'd seen them again, on her way out of the hotel, and told them she was leaving. They seemed to agree that it was for the best. She expected they'd stay out there for the full week they'd planned—at David's expense, actually.

Zoey winced. She was quite glad she was missing that too. And if she was lucky, she'd have found a room in a shared flat or something and moved in before they even realised she'd been staying at home.

She wasn't particularly keen on the idea of going back to flat shares and tiny cramped accommodation after David's luxury apartment, but she didn't have much in the way of choices. She loved her job, but her salary didn't stretch far in London. And part of going it alone meant she really couldn't ask her parents for help, beyond a bed for a few nights while they were away.

She'd make it work. She always had before.

Stretching out her legs, Zoey stared across the airport terminal at all the holiday-makers coming and going. Happy families, loved-up couples, honeymooners, retirees, excited kids…all living the lives she wanted for herself. All with someone or a whole family of someones to love and support them.

And here she was, alone with her coffee and a sense of impending doom.

'This has to be rock-bottom,' she whispered to herself.

Then she straightened her back. Because if this was as low as she could get, that meant the only way forward was up.

Yanking her phone from her pocket, she opened up the notes app and started to type.

New Plan for Fewer Disasters

No disasters seemed a little ambitious, but fewer was surely doable.

1) Take responsibility for my own life and future.
2) Decide what I want from life that I can give myself, without needing some-one else.
3) Quit dating for a while. Say, six months, minimum.
4) Say no next time someone proposes to me. Just for a change.

Hopefully number three would make number four a moot point for a while, but it still felt good to have it down there. Because it might have taken her a while, but she was finally ready to admit that marriage wasn't the be-all and end-all she'd always treated it as.

Yes, she still hoped to have that happy marriage and family life one day. But she was done putting off all the other life she could be living while she searched for it.

From now on, she was living *her* best life, on her own, on her terms.

And she didn't need anyone else to make that happen for her.

Zoey smiled. It felt good to be in control for once.

As the first boarding call for her plane went out, she stood in the queue, her bag at her feet, and started another list on her phone.

Zoey's Best Life List

Now she had hours in the air to think of fantastically fun things to add to it.

Things that definitely weren't *Sleep with Ash Carmichael again.*

CHAPTER NINE

HIS TRIP TO paradise was most definitely over, Ash decided, as he stared at the pile of paperwork sitting on his desk a week later. He'd headed back to the London office via a few other properties he needed to check, fully expecting to be sent straight back out on location to check on one of Carmichael's other existing or potential properties somewhere around the globe. But instead he'd returned to find expenses needing to be filed, reports to be typed up and his assistant absent without leave.

Plus, he was still thinking about Zoey.

She'd texted to tell him she'd arrived home safely, but that was all he'd heard from her since he'd put her on the boat to the mainland. No video call to check in, no funny emails about what she was up to, no new address details, not even a group chat inviting him out for drinks if he was in town this weekend.

Nothing.

It was making him anxious.

Maybe he'd call her tonight, if he wasn't preparing to fly straight back out again, as normal. They could have dinner, like they'd talked about. That would be good. And hopefully not too awkward.

Sinking into his swivel chair, he thumbed idly through the stack in his in-tray and considered how the paperless office had never truly evolved. He'd dealt with all his emails while he was away, like always, but somehow that never quite covered everything that came up in a business day.

And there were no trips scheduled in his calendar. No flights booked or e-tickets waiting for him.

For the first time in two years, since he'd returned to work after Grace's death, he had nowhere to go.

He couldn't help but think this was some

sort of a hint. And probably a sign he should go and talk to his father.

Or Zoey.

But no, his father first.

Wandering past his assistant's empty desk, he moved down the corridor, past wide windows showcasing the London skyline, towards the biggest office in the building. The office belonging to Arthur Carmichael, CEO of Carmichael Luxury Travel and very much still in situ as head of the company even at nearly seventy.

'Is he in?' Ash asked Moira, his dad's long-suffering assistant.

She nodded sagely, as if she knew something Ash didn't. Which she probably did.

Many things, actually. It was a standing joke that Moira knew the jobs of everyone else in the company better than they did.

'He's waiting for you,' she said with a sympathetic smile.

Oh. That didn't sound good.

Ash gave a perfunctory knock on the office door, then stuck his head around it. 'Dad?'

'Ash! Come in, son.' His father seemed in a reasonably jolly mood at least, Ash observed as he carefully shut the door behind him. He was still apprehensive as he took a seat, however.

It definitely felt as if he was missing something here.

'What can I do for you?' Arthur settled back into his seat, folding his arms against his chest as he leaned back, studying his son across the large mahogany desk.

'I was just checking in, really,' Ash said. 'Um, like I said in my email, the refurbishments on that one villa weren't complete, but I can go back in a few more weeks when they are. And, uh, I don't suppose you've seen my assistant, have you?'

It would help, Ash thought, if he could remember his assistant's name. But, in his defence, he'd only met her a couple of times. He'd not exactly spent a lot of time in the office lately. And her email address only had her initials… *R*, he thought. Rachel? Rebecca?

'Ruth has been reassigned,' Arthur said ca-

sually. 'Really, she was far too highly qual-
ified to be just booking your flights and
submitting your expenses.'

'But wasn't that sort of her job?' Ash asked,
confused.

'Assistant to the company's second-in-
command?' Arthur asked, his eyebrows
raised. 'I rather think she was hoping to be a
little more involved, don't you?'

This wasn't about Ruth at all, Ash realised
suddenly. It was about *him*.

He was the one who hadn't been involved.
Who hadn't spent more than a night or two
in London in two years.

Because London was where he'd lost Grace.

He'd been coasting along on his grief ever
since, taking every opportunity to fly away,
stay away. And yes, he was working—but
that wasn't why he'd been doing it. Not for
the company. For the escape.

'Ash, your mother and I know the last two
years have been unbearable for you.' Arthur
bent forward, resting his forearms on the desk
as he looked Ash in the eye. Ash made him-

self hold his father's gaze, however much he wanted to look away. 'And I appreciate that you needed time to grieve, to cope and move on. We've tried to accommodate that as best we can within the company. But your mother and I both think it's time, son. Time to come back to us. Not just to work, but to *yourself.* Stop running away and start moving towards something again.'

'So you reassigned my assistant?' Ash raised an eyebrow. 'Mum told you to talk to me about my personal life, so you gave Ruth a new job?' How like his father to make the personal professional.

'I figured taking away the person who booked the plane tickets might be the only way to keep you in the country long enough to talk to me,' Arthur said.

Ash looked away, conceding the point.

'It's just…been easier to be away, for a while,' Ash admitted. Then he thought about Zoey, picking herself up and starting over after the latest self-imposed implosion of her love life. She moved on, every time. Maybe his dad was right. Maybe it was time for him to do the same. He straightened up and caught his father's gaze. 'But I'm back now. And I'm ready to get back to doing the real work. Not just the busy work or travelling around checking on things that don't need checking on.'

A slow smile spread across Arthur's face. 'Well, that's good. Because I am rather hoping to retire one day, you know. And if you want to take this place over, we've got two years' worth of work to catch you up on.'

Looked like dinner with Zoey would have to wait. 'Let's get started, then.'

Zoey stared at the pregnancy test in her hand and forced herself to acknowledge the information it was giving her.

Outside the bathroom door, she could hear her two new roommates having a row about who had drunk the last of the vodka the night before. She tried to tune it out as she focused on the word in front of her.

Pregnant.

It said it right there in actual letters and

everything. No *Is that one line or two?* or *Do you think that's really a cross?* questions about it.

And it wasn't the only one. She had three other tests that all said exactly the same thing.

She was pregnant.

She, Zoey Hepburn, disaster magnet extraordinaire, was going to be a mother.

Just when she was starting to get a handle on things.

She'd put off taking the test for as long as she could, but by the time she was three weeks late she hadn't even really needed the confirmation of the test. Her cycle might have been unpredictable since she came off the Pill, but not *that* unpredictable. And as much as she'd tried to ignore the exhaustion, the aching breasts and the nausea she felt in the early evening, she'd known what they meant—even if she hadn't been ready to confirm it until now.

Zoey tucked the test into the bottom of the bin, along with the other two. She didn't need anyone else finding out about this before she'd figured out what it meant for herself. Five weeks since she'd run out on her wedding. Five weeks since she'd decided to take control of her life and fight for the future she wanted and could make for herself.

And now this.

Zoey swallowed as tears burned behind her eyes. She'd only had four weeks of managing any semblance of a responsible grown-up life on her own. How could she possibly manage a newborn too?

She shook her head. There was no point whining about it. She'd made a vow to own her mistakes and take responsibility for her choices.

And she knew one thing for certain. No child was a mistake.

This was her baby. So she'd take responsibility for it. She'd love it and care for it and... and she should probably stop calling him or her *it* too, even in her head. She might give it—them?—a complex.

'We're going to be all right,' she whispered in the vague direction of her navel. 'I'm...

well, I have no idea how yet, but we are. I've screwed up enough times that I have to start getting things right eventually, yeah?'

Okay. So she knew nothing about babies. Or pregnancy. But she could find out. The Internet held all the secrets and one of the things she *had* managed to do in the last four weeks was find a flat with actual functioning Wi-Fi. And nightmare roommates, admittedly, but she could stay in her bedroom and Internet search.

There would be websites and lists that she could read and take notes from. She could figure out everything she needed to do, then break it down into manageable chunks and just do it. One small baby step at a time, so it didn't overwhelm her completely.

Easy.

Except…except the first thing on any list had to be telling the father, right?

Ash.

It could only be his. She and David hadn't had sex for over six weeks before the wedding—and even then she'd still been on the

Pill. This baby could only be the result of her one unplanned, irresponsible night of passion with Ash.

She'd been avoiding him ever since they'd got back. No, not avoiding him. Just not going out of her way to see him. He was probably off jetting around the world as usual, anyway. He hadn't used to travel so much for work, that she remembered. But, ever since Grace died, he'd seemed to enjoy the excuse to get away. He'd even sold the house they'd bought when they'd married, buying a soulless flat somewhere fancy along the river, where he hardly ever spent any time. More often he'd been in her flat instead, especially when David was out.

But not since their return from paradise. She hadn't even told him her new address.

But she'd promised him she'd tell him if there were any…side-effects from their night together. And of course she would. Just not yet.

She wasn't ready. She needed more time to figure things out.

Like how she was going to cope with a baby on her own.

Zoey sank back down onto the toilet seat and tried to imagine telling him. Finding the actual words to let Ash know he was going to be a father, after all.

Oh, God, it would break him, she realised suddenly.

He'd had his true love, his chance at a family—and it had been cruelly taken from him. To offer him this now would be some poor substitute.

But this was his baby too. One thing she couldn't do alone, because she didn't have the right to. She couldn't cut him out of his own child's life that way.

She knew Ash, knew the way he thought, the codes he lived by. He'd do everything he could to support her and love their child, she had no doubt about that. And she wanted their baby to have him actively involved in his or her life. She'd never deny her child or her friend those things.

But she had to protect herself too.

If she was going to do this—have a baby with Ash Carmichael—she had to be very clear on what that meant and what it didn't mean.

But first she had to tell him.

Taking a deep breath, Zoey grabbed her phone and tapped out a text.

Are you in town? It would be good to catch up...

Ash smiled at the screen in front of him. Finally Zoey had got in touch. The message was just like the ones she normally sent when she fancied a night out, away from David usually. Obviously she'd meant what she'd said when she'd told him she wanted to pretend their time on the island had never happened.

She'd probably been waiting, he realised, until she was sure there were no consequences to their night together. If there had been, she'd have been in touch before now. He'd had an anxious couple of nights a few weeks ago, after some date-counting on the calendar. He couldn't know *exactly* when Zoey would be able to test if she was pregnant or not, but he'd done enough research on the subject to narrow it down. So he'd sat in his office, staring blankly at the computer screen, waiting to hear from her—but there had been nothing. Nothing except a strange sense of loss as the weeks passed—which Ash had tried to bury in work and ignore.

The bottom line was, Zoey would have got in touch sooner if there was anything he needed to know, he was sure. She wouldn't keep it from him. So she wasn't pregnant. That was good. Right?

Which meant they could just get back to being friends again. Perfect.

Picking up his phone, Ash tapped out a reply.

I am, as it happens. Want to get together tonight? I'll pick you up at seven. What's your new address?

No point giving her a chance to opt out, now they'd got this far.

He hadn't seen his best friend in weeks and he missed her.

Most of that was his fault, he knew. He could have got in touch with her as easily as she had with him. But it turned out that not travelling didn't mean not being busy. His father had declared it time for a future planning meeting and dragged him, Moira and a variety of other essential staff off to the family manor house in Kent for several days of meetings and discussions about the direction the business should be taking next.

And then Arthur had casually dumped the whole thing in Ash's lap.

'You're the future of the company, not me. So this is your project. Stay here, or go and actually live in that fancy apartment on the Thames you bought. I don't care. Just get on with it.'

Then he'd left before Ash had even had a chance to object.

Not that he really wanted to. Suddenly, for the first time in two years, he was excited to be working again. Really working—not just escaping from his real life, or his memories. He had a purpose again, and it felt good to be getting stuck in. Even being back in London had been bearable—he felt as if he'd moved on to a different world, a different life. Starting over, just like Zoey was.

Suddenly, an unwelcome thought hit him. What if he was just replacing one sort of escape with another? He'd thrown himself into work and told himself that he was moving on, but he had to admit that the distraction it provided had been welcome too.

Because when he wasn't working, he was thinking about Zoey. Remembering that last moment they'd been alone on the beach together, before the boat had rescued them. Picturing her naked body beside him, sure, but more than that.

He kept remembering that unreadable look he'd seen on her face. The one that told him he was missing something. That there was something wrong, something she wasn't telling him.

Something, he reluctantly admitted to himself, that he was too scared to ask about again.

But maybe he didn't have to. Maybe they could just go back to being friends.

Starting tonight.

Pulling up his web browser, Ash started searching for somewhere fun to take her. Something *she* would enjoy. Something that would show her she was still important to him—just in a friendly way.

His phone pinged.

Pick me up at work?

The gallery. Ash frowned. Was that because she was still staying with her parents and didn't want a scene, or because she didn't think he'd approve of wherever she'd moved to next?

He'd figure it out later. Everything would be easier once they were spending time together again, talking again.

And her text had just helped him find the perfect place to take her too.

CHAPTER TEN

ZOEY STARED AT the three dresses she'd brought to work at the gallery with her and tried to decide which one put across her message best. Of course, it would be helpful if her message was less confusing.

Mother of your child, best friend and occasional lover, but that's all stopping now and we're just friends and co-parents from here on out was a lot of stress to put on any outfit.

At least she wasn't showing yet. Well, apart from being a bit more bloated than usual, but she doubted Ash would be looking closely enough to notice that. He might spot her swollen breasts though… Zoey took down the lowest cut of the three dresses from the rail in the back office, discounting it from her decision-making process.

If only all decisions were so easy. Like trying to figure out exactly how to tell Ash that she was pregnant.

Sighing, Zoey closed her eyes, turned around once, then grabbed the first dress her hand hit—a navy blue tunic-style thing she'd bought in a sale and never worn, for some reason. Perfect. It would cover any bloat bump *and* her enhanced cleavage. He'd never notice a thing.

Once the gallery was closed for the night, she changed and did her make-up in the washroom mirror, glad to have peace and quiet to get ready alone. As soon as she'd read Ash's text about picking her up she'd known she couldn't invite him back to her current flat share. If her roommates weren't at each other's throats, then the state of the place would be enough to make him turn up his nose. Zoey had tried to keep things clean, at least, but it was an ongoing battle, given the slobs she was living with.

Another thing to fix before the baby came. She had to find somewhere better to live. Although how she was going to do that on her wages—especially once she was on maternity leave—she had no idea. The gallery's HR policies were a little lacking in that area, she'd discovered during her lunch break. Statutory Maternity Pay was the best she could hope for after the first few months. And if she had to pay nursery fees as well as rent...

One problem at a time, she reminded herself, as her breathing grew shallow and panicked. *First, tell Ash. Then panic about everything else.*

One thing was becoming abundantly clear the more she read up and looked into her options—her plans to go it alone, to be solely responsible for her own life, were suddenly a hell of a lot harder. Like it or not, she was going to have to swallow her pride and ask Ash for help if she wanted to keep her head above water.

And he'd give it, she had no doubt of that. She just worried what the cost would be to her heart.

At precisely seven o'clock Zoey heard a light tap on the gallery's glass door and, turning out the last of the lights and grabbing her bag and keys, she headed out to meet Ash, her chest tight and her shoulders tense.

This was it. And no dress in the world could make it any easier.

'Hey.' With a broad smile, Ash ducked his head to brush a kiss against her cheek. 'You look…lovely.'

Zoey's own smile stiffened. Had he noticed something? Or was he just awkward because the last time they'd been together she'd mostly been naked?

She wished she could just blurt it out now and get it over with, but Ash deserved to hear the news of his impending fatherhood somewhere a little more salubrious than a darkened London backstreet.

'Where's the restaurant?' she asked as he led her away from the gallery. She hoped it was close—if she'd known they'd be walking she'd have worn lower shoes.

He flashed her a secretive grin. 'No restaurant—well, not yet, anyway. We can grab dinner later. And there's bound to be canapés at this thing if you're really hungry.'

'What thing?' Zoey asked, her shoulders practically up around her ears with tension. They were supposed to be going to a restaurant. Preferably a quiet and discreet one where she could tell him her news in private. 'Where are we going?'

From his jacket pocket, Ash pulled out two tickets and waved them under her nose. 'You know that exhibition at the Hemmingslea Gallery everyone's been talking about? I got us tickets to the opening tonight.'

He looked so pleased with himself, so sure he'd done a good thing, that there was no way Zoey could tell him that, actually, the thought of standing up and making polite conversation with art-lovers for the next couple of hours made her miserable. Besides, that opening had been sold out for weeks, and it was definitely something Ash must have pulled some serious strings to get—because he knew *she'd* enjoy it. He'd never cared what everyone was talking about anyway, and the art world wasn't exactly his natural habitat.

He'd done this for her. So Zoey plastered on a smile and said, 'That's brilliant! Thank you,' as genuinely as she could manage.

She just hoped she didn't throw up over any priceless works of art.

Something was up with Zoey.

It had taken him a while to notice; she'd seemed fine at the gallery earlier, and gratifyingly excited by the tickets he'd managed to procure. But his first clue should have been the dress. It was dark and boring, and totally un-Zoey-like.

For a moment, he'd wondered if she'd gone out and bought something plain and loose cut to make sure he didn't get any ideas about how the night would end. Then he'd reminded himself that tonight was about rebuilding their friendship—not rekindling whatever they'd shared that night on the island. It probably hadn't even occurred to her. Maybe she was just going for a new look.

Anyway, the point was, he'd dismissed the dress from his mind. And then he'd been so enjoying spending time with her again, filling her in on his latest project at the company, how exciting it was to be moving on finally, finding his feet in the world again— that it had taken longer than it should to notice that Zoey wasn't her normal, sparkling self on their walk to the Hemmingslea Gallery.

As they wandered around the exhibition opening night party, however, there was no denying it.

Something's wrong.

As soon as he knew that, he could see the signs of it in every movement she made. The fixed smile on her pale face. The way she gripped onto a nearby chair too tightly, turning down a glass of champagne for the third time. The slightly green tinge she developed as another waiter brought round a tray of prawn canapés.

'Are you feeling okay?' he asked as she shook her head at the waiter.

'I'm fine,' she replied. But her smile didn't reach her eyes.

Maybe she was *physically* fine, Ash decided, but that didn't mean that there wasn't something else going on.

She was avoiding alcohol—because she was afraid that if they got drunk together again they'd make the same mistake they had on the island? Was she looking so stiff and was the conversation so stilted and one-sided because she still felt awkward around him?

Or was there something else?

Whatever it was, they definitely needed to talk about it. And not surrounded by priceless art and hundreds of other people, preferably.

'Where did you fancy for dinner?' he asked casually, hoping to build up to leaving early.

Zoey's eyes widened and the green tinge got stronger. 'Sorry. Be right back.'

And she was gone, through the crowds, towards the cloakroom.

Okay, she definitely wasn't fine, whatever she said. And there was something, a niggling feeling at the back of his head, that told him he knew what the problem was.

No. She'd have told me by now.

Following at a slower pace, Ash made his way over to the cloakrooms, where the girl who'd welcomed them waited, guarding jackets and bags.

'Did you see a beautiful woman in a navy dress come this way?'

She smiled and nodded towards the ladies' bathroom.

That made sense. At least she hadn't run out on him completely. That was always a risk with Zoey.

Leaning against the wall, Ash waited until she emerged again, still pale but less green.

'Want to try telling me you're fine again?' he asked, pushing away from the wall. 'Or do you fancy trying the truth this time?'

'Ash, really. I'm fine. Must have been something I ate disagreeing with me.' Another person might have found her words and her smile convincing—someone who didn't know Zoey as well as he did.

But he'd seen that look in her eyes before, and recently. That haunted, hunted look, as if she was desperately searching for an escape route, a way to run.

It was the same look she'd had when he'd found her in a cupboard, trying to climb out of a window to avoid marrying David.

The fact she now displayed the same look and feel in relation to *him* was a stab to Ash's heart—and his pride.

'Don't lie to me, Zoey,' he said, his voice low. 'I'm not some fiancé you're running out on. I'm your friend. I want to help you. And I can't do that if you won't tell me the truth.'

'You want to help...' Zoey shook her head as she looked down at the floor, giving a low laugh. 'And I know I need your help. I just... I was so determined to do it on my own. And the moment I tell you, that's over. You'll want to fix everything for me.'

Fix everything. That meant there was something that needed fixing. *Of course* he was going to want to do that, then.

'Zo. Please. Just talk to me.'

Indecision flickered across her face. 'Not here,' she said finally. 'I want to tell you—I've been trying to figure out how all night. But not here.'

Grabbing his hand, she pulled him out of the main foyer and into a small side gallery he'd had no idea was even there.

The room was mostly in darkness—the rest of the gallery was closed for the evening, and Ash was pretty sure they weren't supposed to be there. But there was just enough light from the foyer for him to see her face as she looked up at him, chewing her lower lip.

'Just tell me,' he whispered. 'Whatever it is, Zo, we can fix it. Together.'

Zoey took a breath so deep he could see her chest rising. And he knew in that moment exactly what was coming next. But somehow he still wasn't prepared for it.

'Ash, I'm pregnant.'

And his whole world shifted again.

Relief settled over her the moment the words were out. She hadn't wanted to tell him here, or like this. But, however it had happened, she was glad that he knew. Glad that she wasn't keeping this secret alone any longer.

Glad that Ash knew he was going to be a father.

'That's why you messaged today? To tell me?' Ash asked, and she nodded. 'And how long have *you* known? Because I figured, when I didn't hear anything weeks ago…'

Zoey winced. 'I know. I'm sorry. But I couldn't work up the courage to take a test until this morning. I texted you as soon as I knew.'

Ash nodded, still looking poleaxed. She couldn't blame him. She still felt much the same way.

'So it's definitely… God, no. I'm not even asking that. Of course it is. You wouldn't be telling me otherwise.'

'Yes, it's yours,' Zoey confirmed for him anyway. 'No doubts there. Abstinence thing before the wedding, remember?'

'Right. Sure.' Ash ran a hand through his dark hair, his pale blue eyes still wide and wild beneath it. He shouldn't look so gorgeous right now, Zoey thought. Or at least she shouldn't be noticing it. There were kind of weightier matters to deal with. But it seemed her libido—or her heart—didn't care so much about those.

She stepped forward and placed a hand on his arm, looking up into his handsome, dear face. 'I'm sorry, Ash.'

Her words seemed to snap something in him as he shook his head firmly.

'You have *nothing* to be sorry for,' he said, his voice low and harsh. 'We were both there on that island together. I take my half of the responsibility too. And even then, it's a *baby,* Zoey. *Our* baby. We made a new life together. Neither one of us should ever have to apologise for that.'

Our baby. For the first time since she'd seen the word forming on the stick that morning, some of the tension drained out of Zoey's shoulders. She wasn't alone with this any longer.

Maybe we humans weren't made to do ev-

erything alone, anyway. Which didn't mean she was ready to give up her plan for taking care of herself. But it wasn't just her now, was it?

And it was kind of a relief to let Ash shoulder some of the responsibility from here on out.

'Are you okay?' He was close, Zoey realised suddenly. Very close. His hands held onto her upper arms as he studied her, but there was none of the lust and want she'd seen there last time they'd been together. Instead, he held her almost delicately, as if he were afraid he might break her. 'With the pregnancy, I mean. Have you seen a doctor yet? No, you only took the test this morning. Well, that's first up, I guess?'

Zoey nodded mutely, unsure how much he actually needed her to contribute to this conversation.

'And Zoey—' those pale blue eyes held hers in their gaze, steady and sure and reassuring '—you're never on your own in this, okay? I'm here, for whatever you need.'

The nausea was starting to rise up again, as if now she was *officially* pregnant the morning sickness needed to up its game. 'Mostly I think I need to get out of here,' she admitted. 'Can you take me home?'

'No,' Ash said, smiling incongruously. 'Because if home was somewhere you were happy to be you'd have let me pick you up from there this evening.'

Zoey winced. 'I'll find somewhere new before the baby comes,' she promised.

'*We'll* find somewhere else,' he corrected. 'In fact, you already have somewhere else. Move in with me.'

'Ash...'

'I mean it. It's the obvious solution.'

She knew that he meant it; that wasn't the problem. But the idea of being there with him all day, every day, living in his space... How was she meant to keep resisting him if he was that close?

Another wave of nausea flowed over her and she realised the whole resisting thing might be easier than she'd thought if that carried on. Those damn prawns. She'd felt fine until a waiter had waved a tray of prawns under her nose. She was never eating seafood again.

'We need a plan, Zo,' he said, more softly. 'We've got, what, seven months or so to figure out how we're going to do this together. So we need to start now, right?'

'With me moving in?' Zoey shook her head. 'I think there have to be a few other steps we can cover first, don't you?' Stalling, that was the key. Until she felt less awful and could think rationally about all this.

Because right now the only part of her brain that was working was screaming for her to just let go and let Ash take care of her. And she was very afraid she might start listening to it soon.

'You're right,' Ash said, unexpectedly. But he was already signalling to the cloakroom attendant over her shoulder, asking for their coats. 'We've lots of things to talk about. So let's head back to my place and talk.'

'Ash...'

'There are no prawns, I promise,' he said, and she looked up at him suddenly. 'You turned green when the waiter brought those out. I think I started to guess then.'

'I hate seafood,' she muttered again.

'Just…come home with me tonight, Zoey. Please. Come home with me, I'll make you a peppermint tea to soothe your stomach and we'll talk as much or as little as you want. Okay?'

And really, how was a girl supposed to turn down an offer like that? The cloakroom girl's expression made it very clear that if Zoey didn't want to take him up on it, she would.

She was tired. She felt sick. And she really wanted someone to lean on for a while.

She wanted her best friend.

'Okay,' Zoey said, hoping she wouldn't regret it later.

CHAPTER ELEVEN

ASH HAD SPENT more time in his London flat over the last month than in the whole two years before, since he'd bought it. Still, opening the door and stepping inside now, with Zoey behind him, it was as if he were seeing it for the first time again.

The white, sleek flooring. The modern black kitchen, open-plan to the black-and-white themed lounge and dining area. There was no colour here, he realised suddenly. How had he never noticed that before?

He turned, expecting to see Zoey in her usual bright hues, but found that damn navy dress again, and an uncertain look on her face that made him nervous.

He needed to convince her to stay. And looking at the place he laughingly called his home, even he couldn't see any reasons why she would.

'I don't think I've ever actually been here, you know.' She stepped inside, looking around her curiously.

'Let's be honest, I've barely ever been here.' He felt as if he wanted to make excuses for the place. To promise that when the baby came there'd be softer edges and brighter colours.

Although just having Zoey there made everything feel softer and brighter, anyway.

As she settled herself on one of the high kitchen stools—and he resisted the urge to tell her to get down in case she fell and hurt the baby, because he knew it was irrational, but that didn't stop him thinking about it— he fixed her a peppermint tea and an ordinary cup for himself. Tea was soothing. Tea would help.

'So.' Zoey looked him directly in the eye over her mug. 'How do you want to do this?'

Ash knew *exactly* how they should do this. But before he got a chance to tell her, Zoey kept on talking.

'I mean, I assume you want to be involved in the baby's life, right? Not just one of those dads who sends money but never sees them. Not that I'm after your money or anything, but obviously it would help. But I can do it alone if I have to. And I know you travel a lot for work, so I'm not expecting that you'll suddenly become a stay-at-home dad or anything. But I would like to keep working, after my maternity leave, so there's that. And I know I need to move flats, and I guess there are probably a few things to change around here before the baby comes too. But basically, whatever involvement you want, I can work with, I think.'

'I want us to get married,' Ash said bluntly, the moment she stopped for breath.

Zoey's whole body jerked away from him so fast he reached out to grab her in case she really did fall off the stool.

'No.' The word came out on a sharp wave of disbelief and anger that Ash couldn't quite understand.

'Why not? It's perfect. You can move in

here—or…or we can find somewhere new together. A proper family home.' Like the one he'd had with Grace. That would have been perfect. 'You'll have all the money you need if you're married to me, we can choose a nanny together so we can both carry on working as we normally do, and whenever I'm home we can be together as a family, without any awkward logistics. I don't see the problem.'

'Apart from the fact that that was the least romantic proposal ever?' Zoey asked, one eyebrow raised. 'Ash, I promised myself, after I left David, that I'd turn down the next proposal that came my way. Because weddings really haven't worked out that well for me in the past, remember?'

'But this one would be different.' Ash grabbed her hands and held them against his chest, staring down into her eyes as he tried to convince her.

This was his one shot, he realised. His one shot to live the life he'd thought had been ripped from him for ever. His chance at a future worth living—not through the company or money or a fancy flat. But with a woman he adored and a child they could raise together.

His one chance at a family again. And there was no one on earth he'd rather do it with.

'Zoey, this time we know what we're getting into. We *know* each other, better than you ever knew any of those guys you ran out on, I reckon. And we know what we're signing up for. This isn't some hopeful fairy-tale ending. This is something better. It's a family. You, me and our child.'

'Ash...'

'I can't promise you true love,' he said, his gaze darting away to the floor as he remembered why. 'You know that. But really, what good has that quest ever done you anyway? Yes, we both know it exists, but we also know it's rare as hens' teeth and that not everyone gets to experience it. But we could have *this*. Together.'

He slid off his stool to hold her closer, feeling her heartbeat racing against his chest. 'You're my best friend, Zoey. There's no one in the world I'd rather raise a child with. No other woman I'd want in my life the way I want you there. You're it for me now.'

There was a tiny sob. Was she crying? And was it too much to hope that it was tears of happiness?

He had to take the chance that it was. His heart thumping in his chest, Ash dropped to his knees, still holding her hands, and looked up.

'Zoey Hepburn, will you give my life meaning again and marry me?'

She swallowed, hard enough that he could see her throat bob, tears drying on her cheeks.

'Yes. I will.'

And Ash's world slid back into focus again.

There was a strong chance that Zoey might have made a terrible mistake.

As she surveyed Ash's apartment, her suitcase at her feet, she wondered if it was too late to back out now. Then she remembered the vintage ring on her finger, and the baby growing inside her, and realised that too late was about two months ago already.

The problem wasn't that she didn't want to marry Ash. It was that she was a bit afraid she wanted it too much.

'Is this really everything?' Ash asked as he lugged another suitcase through the door.

Zoey shrugged. 'I move often. I learned to travel light.'

Her whole life in two suitcases. She'd packed up and started again so many times now that she only kept the essentials. Every wedding she ran out on was a chance to slim down her possessions, if nothing else.

'I'll put these in your room, then.' He grabbed the other case—which she hadn't been allowed to carry up the stairs either—and headed in the direction of the bedrooms.

Your room. Not *our room.* Another reminder that this wasn't a real marriage.

Ash had been, as predicted, horrified by her flat share. And Zoey had to admit, as she sank down onto one of his black leather couches to look out over the London skyline, the view was much better from here. She was sure the place would start to feel homelier in time, anyway. Even if she still felt garishly out of place in her pink and white sundress.

The biggest problem was that *this*—the luxury flat, Ash carrying her suitcases—definitely wasn't doing things by herself.

She sighed, and made herself remember all the reasons she'd agreed to this.

It wasn't as if she hadn't followed through and said no the first time he'd proposed, anyway. But the second time…he'd painted such a perfect picture of their future together, she'd known that they could be happy together.

Although possibly happier if they were sharing the same bedroom…

The point was, she had a future now. A plan. And, more importantly, so did her child. And so did Ash.

This could be the last chance either of them had to find that kind of happiness—together. And while it might not be the happily-ever-after she'd been searching for, she had to admit it was pretty damn good.

Ash wanted this. Wanted her, and their child.

And when he'd looked at her, that longing in his eyes for something he'd never thought he could have again, that was when she'd realised.

She could never turn him down. Couldn't tear his life apart again and steal away that future once more.

Because she was in love with him.

Properly, truly, happily-ever-after love. And she knew he'd never be able to give her that back, but maybe that was okay. Maybe one of them feeling that way was enough.

He respected her, adored her, even wanted her still, she hoped. He was her best friend and he *did* love her, she knew. Just not *that* way.

But love was love. And when that love offered a future, a family, happiness, she was going to take it. For herself, as much as for Ash.

And for the baby. Because he or she was the most important thing in this whole situation now. And she knew that being with Ash would be the best outcome for their child, by far.

'Want to see your room?' Ash's head popped back into the room from the hallway, and Zoey pasted on a smile.

'Definitely.'

As she followed him down past the main bathroom, she realised suddenly that there were *three* bedrooms down there.

'Mine's the one at the end,' Ash said, waving a hand. 'And I've put your stuff in here, if that's okay?'

Zoey nodded. But she was still looking at the third door, slightly ajar. 'What's in there?'

Was Ash *blushing*? 'Oh, well, I didn't want to do too much—I was pretty sure you'd have opinions on design and furniture and stuff. But...' He pushed the door fully open, and Zoey smiled.

The room was bright and sunny, obviously recently repainted in a warm and welcoming yellow. A silver-grey carpet had been put down over the hard white concrete floor. And hanging from the ceiling was a mobile, tiny planets and moons dangling from invisible strings.

'We can change any of it you want,' Ash said nervously. 'I just thought it would be good to have some things in place to start.'

He'd built the baby a nursery. Never mind her room, *this* was what she'd needed to see to be sure.

She flung her arms around him and hugged him tight. 'Thank you.'

'Anything for you,' he murmured into her hair. 'And the baby.'

And suddenly Zoey was sure that she wasn't making a mistake at all.

Everything was going to work out just right.

Ash stirred the pot on the hob and tried to remember if he'd ever actually cooked here before—something more than reheating last night's takeaway. Possibly not.

But now Zoey was here, everything was different. And she'd wanted Italian chicken, just like the one they'd eaten in a restaurant round the corner last week. Figuring that home-cooked food had to be good for the baby—even if it *was* cooked by him—Ash had finagled the recipe from the chef and was attempting to recreate it for her.

In the two weeks since she'd moved in, Ash's whole world seemed to have changed. It wasn't just the splashes of colour that filled his flat these days—a bright pink scarf left draped over the back of a chair, or a royal purple cardigan hung on the back of the door, or even the scent of Zoey's lavender perfume, lingering in a room after she'd gone to bed. It was the whole feel of the place. Hearing her humming to herself as she made them coffee in the morning—decaf for her, full strength for him—or watching her, feet kicked up under her on the sofa, as she leafed through an art catalogue she'd brought home from work. Suddenly, with the addition of an extra person in his life—two, if you counted the baby, and he did—his functional apartment felt like a home.

Yes, Ash was pretty sure that asking Zoey to marry him was the best thing he'd done in years.

Except they hadn't really moved on any further than agreeing to get married in the first place. Oh, he'd bought her a ring—a vintage sapphire and diamond ring, set in white gold, that he'd spotted in an antique shop on his way home one night and just known, without any hesitation at all, was meant to be on Zoey's finger. From the way her face had lit up as he'd presented it to her over Chinese takeaway that night, he'd been right.

But that was as far as they'd got. And time was moving on. If they wanted to get married before the baby came, they'd needed to get moving. Venues were probably already booked up, and dresses took forever to alter, he seemed to remember. Zoey would know what they needed to do. She was the wedding expert, after all—not that he planned to mention that to her.

Putting the lid on the pot to let the chicken

simmer in the sauce, he crossed over to perch on the arm of the sofa Zoey was sitting on.

'Hey,' he said softly, drawing her attention away from the catalogue. 'I was thinking. We should start making plans—for the wedding, I mean.'

She gave a small shrug and smiled at him. 'I guess. I figured we'd just see what dates the registry office had free and go with that?'

Ash blinked. He'd been invited to five of Zoey's non-weddings so far—well, four if you discounted Harry, since the invitations were never actually posted for that one. Not one of them had taken place at a registry office. There'd been two in churches, one in a pagoda by a stream, one in some swanky hotel in central London, then the one out in the Indian Ocean that had brought them here.

The one thing they all had in common was, whoever she was intending to marry, Zoey planned to put on a show. A big display of love and happiness for everyone to share in. Not because she was trying to show off—he knew that wasn't her style. Just because she wanted her big day to be a big deal.

In her mind, it was always the start of the rest of her life. 'And I want to start it off with a bang!' she'd told him once, when he'd asked about the fireworks on a village green some-where, outside the perfect stone church.

But this time, marrying him, she was plan-ning on the registry office? That didn't feel right.

'I thought you might want something a little…fancier?' he said tentatively. 'I mean, you know the money isn't a problem. And if this is the one wedding you actually go through with, I want it to be everything that *you* want.'

Her smile softened as she looked at him fondly. 'Ash, I don't need fancier. I don't need the show this time. A registry office wedding will be more than fine.'

He almost didn't want to ask, but he couldn't stop himself. 'Why? Why is this time so dif-ferent?'

Zoey laughed at that, her face bright. 'Really? Ash, *everything* is different this time. I mean, I'm pregnant, you've been married before, and we're doing this because we're building a family together. It's practical, not romantic. We're not even sleeping in the same bedroom, for heaven's sake. So why make a big deal out of the wedding?'

Her words stung, even as he realised the truth of them. 'That doesn't mean it isn't important. Meaningful.'

She shrugged again. 'And it'll still be meaningful in a registry office, whether I'm wearing a white dress or not. Is that the chicken?'

The sound of the kitchen timer broke through his thoughts at last, and he dashed back to the kitchen to rescue dinner. But he couldn't shake her words.

It's practical, not romantic.

Yes, it was practical. But couldn't it be both? Why did practical have to mean they stripped all the romance away?

He wanted this wedding day to be a fresh start for both of them. A new life together. Not just a piece of paperwork they needed to make the legalities and practicalities of being a family more straightforward.

We're not even sleeping in the same bedroom.

Ash dropped the wooden spoon onto the counter as those words drifted through his mind. Was *that* the problem?

He'd been holding back because he thought that was the right thing to do. She was pregnant, exhausted and nauseous a lot of the time. Plus they'd decided to be friends—but that was before they'd also decided to get married. He hadn't wanted to push the issue of what their physical romantic relationship might be when they were married, choosing to leave it up to her to define that when she felt ready.

But he knew what he wanted. He knew *exactly* what he wanted.

Did she, though?

Did she honestly not realise the battle he fought every day not to grab her and kiss her? The tight hold he'd had to keep on his self-control not to suggest she join him every night when they went to their separate rooms? How crazy it drove him catching her scent everywhere he turned and not being able to hold her close?

Perhaps she didn't.

And perhaps it was time he made that clear.

Ash turned off the heat under the pot. Dinner could wait.

CHAPTER TWELVE

'IS IT READY?' Zoey asked as Ash approached again from the kitchen. She couldn't quite read the look on his face, but suddenly she got the feeling he wasn't coming to talk about the food.

He shook his head, confirming her suspicions. 'I need to talk to you about something first.'

Apprehension filled her, tightening her chest as she closed the catalogue in her hands. 'Okay.' Was he going to call the whole thing off? Tell her it would never work?

That he knew she loved him, and he couldn't ever love her back, so they should forget all this stupid marriage business?

This time, when he sat, Ash chose the seat right next to her and took her hand in his. She hoped he couldn't feel it trembling.

'You said that our wedding was practical. Functional, even.'

'Because it is,' she replied. 'Isn't it?' She couldn't quite keep the hope from her voice, but if Ash heard it he didn't show it.

'I suppose so,' he said. But then one of his hands drifted up her arm, along her neck, cupping her jawline and suddenly breathing became an awful lot harder. 'But that's not all I want it to be.'

Zoey forced herself to swallow down the hope that was building inside her. 'What… what were you hoping for, then?'

'This.' He gave her plenty of time to back away as he bent his head to kiss her. But all Zoey could think was, *At last.*

Oh, she had missed this so much. The feel of his lips against hers, his mouth, his tongue darting out across hers. Missed the heat that rose up to fill her at his touch. His arms, shoulders and back—so steady, hard and strong with muscle—under her fingers. His black hair, silky as she ran her hands through it. And the way he held her close—as if she was precious, but also greedily, as if he'd die if he couldn't have her right now...

Actually, *she* might die if she couldn't have him again. Now.

Ash pulled away and Zoey heard herself whimper at the loss of his lips. *So pathetic, Hepburn.*

'Uh, what I was trying to say...' He trailed off as if the intensity of the kiss had surprised him too.

'I think...' Zoey swallowed as her voice came out croaky, then tried again. 'I think I get what you were saying.'

He gave her a wicked smile, one that lit her up from within again, thinking of the last time she'd seen that smile, on a beach in paradise.

'I was holding back,' he said softly. 'I don't want to rush you into anything, but I'd hate for you to think for a moment that I don't still want you. That when I proposed to you I didn't hope that, one day, we'd have more than just a functional marriage.'

'I want that too,' she whispered. It wasn't

love, of course. But to have Ash with her every day, and in her bed every night? That was close. It could be enough.

Couldn't it?

He kissed her again, lighter and happier, but no less arousing.

'So,' he asked. 'Dinner or bed?'

She didn't even have to think about the answer.

'Bed.'

Later—much later—as they lay in the darkness, Zoey tucked into the crook of his arm as he ran his other hand down her side, Ash wondered how he'd got so damn lucky.

'I never thought I could have all this again, you know,' he whispered to her, not sure if she was even still awake. 'I'm so happy I get to have it with you.'

'So am I,' she whispered back. But there was something in her voice—something that reminded him of her running away from him on that beach in paradise. Something that gave him pause, even while he couldn't put his finger on quite what it was.

'Are you okay?' he asked softly. 'Do you need anything?'

Whatever she needed, he'd give her, if it was within his power.

Zoey wriggled into an upright position, dragging the blanket with her so it covered those magnificent breasts he'd so enjoyed rediscovering. The fact that pregnancy had made them even more sensitive was only a bonus.

'Dinner?' she asked hopefully. 'We never got around to it, and I'm kind of hungry.'

Of course. Ash's worries floated away as he pressed a quick kiss to her lips and jumped out of bed, reaching for his trousers.

'Stay here. I'll bring it to you,' he said, whistling as he headed back to the kitchen.

Everything was going to be fine now. He was sure of it.

The next few weeks disappeared in a rush of wedding preparations and sex.

Zoey held firm on her registry office plan, and eventually even Ash seemed to agree it was the best idea.

'Apart from the fact it's the only way we're going to get this organised in time if you keep dragging me back to bed every time we have a moment free, I quite like it,' she said one Saturday morning as they lay together, naked under the sheets.

'I haven't heard you objecting to the bed part,' Ash commented.

'I'm not. But I am being practical. *And* romantic.'

Ash propped himself up on one elbow as he looked down at her. 'How so?'

Zoey grinned up at him, loving the feel of him so close. 'This wedding is about the future, right? Our lives together, with our child.' Her hand went automatically to her belly as she said it, and bumped into his as it rested there.

'Right,' Ash agreed. 'So?'

'So the actual wedding is the least important part. I'm less interested in the day itself, and more focused on everything that comes next.' His expression softened a little at that and Zoey felt it, tight in her chest. 'Plus, it means we can spend more time in bed and less time looking at venues.'

'I'm always in favour of that,' Ash agreed, swooping down to kiss her again. And then they had better things to do than talk.

Which was just as well, Zoey thought later. Because otherwise she might have ended up confessing her other reasons for wanting to keep things simple.

This wasn't like her other weddings. There was no hope for true love here—as much as she was still holding out for *content and sexually satisfied ever after.* She knew she needed to keep that at the front of her mind. Keeping the wedding to a simple registry office affair and lunch with Ash's parents afterwards was just one of the ways she was doing that.

Her heart ached with the knowledge that the man she loved more than anything in the world would never love her back the same way. He might be her prince, her forever love.

But she'd only ever be his stand-in princess, the understudy in a role she was never meant to play for real.

And she could live with that, she'd decided, for the sake of their child. But she couldn't ever let herself forget her place. Because, if she did, she knew that the smallest reminder would break her, over and over again.

She and Ash loved each other as best friends, and co-parents to be. And as far as he and the rest of the world were to know, that was exactly how things would stay.

No one else needed to know her secret truth.

On the morning of the wedding, Ash kissed her goodbye—a long, lingering promise of a kiss—as she lay in bed. 'I'll see you there, yes?'

She smiled lazily up at him. 'As long as I can bring myself to get out of this bed, yes.' When he still looked a trifle uncertain, she rolled her eyes. 'I'm marrying you today, Ash Carmichael, come hell or high water. So go pick up your parents and I'll see you at the registry office.'

He grinned. 'Okay. Your car will be here in two hours.' Another quick kiss and he was gone.

Zoey took her time getting ready—the plain ivory silk, empire-line dress she'd chosen was loose and flowing around her waist, but dipped deep at the neckline to make the most of her enhanced cleavage. It fell almost to the floor, but stopped just short to show off her bright pink heels. She curled her hair so it fell around her shoulders and applied her normal make-up rather than the extra brides were always recommended to wear, to last out the day.

Her day would end after the wedding lunch. Then, tomorrow, they'd fly out to the South of France for their honeymoon—something Ash had insisted they have, even if they were forgoing most of the other traditional wedding trappings.

'If this day is about starting our lives together, then I want to make sure we start it right,' he'd said.

'You mean by taking me away and keeping me in bed for a week?' Zoey had guessed.

'Exactly,' Ash had replied, with one of his most wicked grins.

Zoey hadn't felt it was worth arguing with, after that.

It felt surreal, preparing for her wedding alone—for all that it was her choice. She hadn't even told her parents she was getting married, this time, let alone about the baby. She'd managed to move out again before they'd even returned from her last wedding, so she hadn't seen them since she'd left the island resort. They hadn't called, and neither had she.

I don't need them now. I've got Ash, and our baby. I've got a new future.

Maybe, if she kept repeating the words to herself, she'd feel less alone.

When the car arrived, the driver called the lift for her and she descended to the street in her wedding dress, waiting for him to open the car door before she got in. As he closed it behind her, she looked to the seat next to her, surprised to find it empty. She'd been expecting to see someone, she realised suddenly. Not her father, or even Ash...

Grace.

The name came to her lips before her brain, almost.

She'd expected to see her best friend since junior school, there on her wedding day to give her away—to give her blessing on her marriage to Ash.

But Grace was gone, and Zoey was alone.

But only until I marry Ash.

The car pulled away from the kerb and Zoey forced herself to focus on the future she'd made for herself—and leave the past behind for good.

CHAPTER THIRTEEN

'WELL, THIS IS a bit different from last time.' Ash's father, Arthur Carmichael, folded his hands behind his back and rose up on the balls of his feet as he surveyed the registry office, before dropping back down again.

'This is still the hallway, Dad,' Ash pointed out. 'I'm sure it's nicer inside.'

His mother had already disappeared to the florist she'd spotted a few doors down, when she'd learned that it was possible Zoey didn't even have a bouquet. He didn't think his parents quite embraced the idea of *simple but meaningful* the way Zoey seemed to have.

To be honest, it wasn't exactly his idea of a dream wedding either.

But he'd already had that once. This was something new. And that was fine.

'I wasn't talking about the venue, son,' Arthur said. 'I meant…this whole thing. Are you sure you really want to do this?'

That, Ash knew for certain. 'Absolutely.'

'For the baby.' Arthur sighed. 'I suppose that's the right thing to do, and your mother will be pleased. But these days, you don't have to, Ash, you know that, yes? You can support her, of course, and be a part of the child's life, without marrying her.'

'I know that.' How could he make his father understand? 'She's…she's my best friend, Dad. I care for her. I want her to be happy. And honestly? She makes me happy too. I never thought I'd find that again.'

'After Grace,' his father said thoughtfully. 'Well, happiness is no bad thing to reach for, I suppose. Even in a place like this. Now, where is your mother? Aren't we supposed to be starting soon?'

'Zoey's not here yet either,' Ash pointed out. 'Don't worry.'

He wasn't worrying. She'd come, he was sure. Things were different this time, after all—wasn't that what she'd said? She could see their future together. He knew her, in a way all those other men she'd almost married didn't. He was her best friend.

She wouldn't let him down.

She'd be there. With or without a bouquet.

He didn't care. As long as she showed up.

'This is a bit different from last time.'

Zoey stopped outside the hallway as she heard Arthur Carmichael speak.

Last time. When Ash had been madly in love with his bride-to-be, and they'd had the perfect wedding and the perfect life.

She shouldn't listen in, she knew that. But she couldn't help herself. And as she heard Ash list the reasons he wanted to go through with the wedding…she couldn't stop herself hoping for words she knew she wouldn't hear.

Because I'm in love with her, Dad.

Of course, they never came.

Because he wasn't in love with her. And he never would be. And she *had* to come to terms with that.

'She makes me happy too. I never thought I'd find that again.'

She made him happy. That was something, wasn't it?

After Grace.

Grace. Grace, who she loved and missed and wished she could see just once more every single day.

Grace, who held Zoey's fiancé's heart and would never give it back.

And so Ash was trying to recreate the future he'd lost, casting Zoey as Grace.

'I can't play that part,' she whispered to herself, realisation washing over her.

She'd known what he'd wanted—the life he'd had torn away from him. She just hadn't realised that she couldn't give it to him.

She couldn't be Grace for him—that wasn't who she was. And she definitely couldn't live knowing he was spending every day comparing her to the wife he'd lost.

She couldn't do this.

She couldn't marry Ash.

Oh, God, she was running out on another wedding.

She turned to leave, only to find Mrs Carmichael rushing up the steps behind her.

'Zoey! Perfect timing. I've brought you these.' She held out a large bunch of yellow roses and Zoey tried not to recoil from the offering.

Not yellow. Yellow is for friendship. She heard Grace's voice in her head as she remembered helping her choose wedding flowers for Ash's *last* wedding.

'That's so kind. Um, could you just hold onto them for me? While I pop to the bathroom? Last-minute make-up check, you know...' She forced a smile, which Ash's mother returned.

'Of course. I'll wait here for you.'

'Lovely,' Zoey said weakly. No chance of escaping back out of the front door now, then.

Zoey hurried down the opposite corridor to where she knew Ash would be waiting, hoping there was a bathroom down there somewhere. Preferably one with a window that opened out onto the street.

* * *

'Ash?'

'Mum! There you are. We were supposed to start ten minutes ago,' Ash said as his mother bustled in carrying a bunch of yellow roses.

'Not that the bride's here yet,' his father put in.

'Yes, she is,' Julia Carmichael said. 'That's what I came to tell you. I saw her ten minutes ago as she came in, and she asked me to hold these for her while she popped to the bathroom. But she never came out!'

Ash's heart began a slow descent into his stomach. *She wouldn't. Would she?*

'I'd go and check on her but, really, I thought it might be better for you to do it, Ash?' his mum went on, looking concerned.

'Definitely better for me to do it,' he agreed. 'Wait here. Don't let them cancel or do *anything* until I get back. Okay?'

His parents nodded, and Ash stalked off towards the nearest ladies' bathroom.

He almost wasn't surprised to see a pair of hot pink high heels discarded by the door.

Or the window above the sink pushed as far open as it would go.

Or even the bride, trying to climb out of it.

'Isn't this where we started?' he asked, keeping a tight hold of his temper. 'With you trying to escape through a window?'

Of course she was running. She was Zoey Hepburn. It was what she did.

Zoey jerked her head around, bashing it on the window frame as she did so. She winced, but didn't cry out. 'Ash…'

'No, don't even start,' he snapped as she climbed down from the counter. 'I know how this song goes—I've heard you sing it enough for others in the past, haven't I? It's not me; it's you. As if I didn't already know that.'

'Hey,' Zoey said sharply. 'Will you give me a chance to explain?'

'Like you intended to give me a chance to convince you before you climbed out of a window?' Ash shook his head. 'I can't honestly believe that I really thought I was different. That we were going to have some perfect life together. When the truth is I'm just like all the other men you ran out on, aren't I?'

'No! Ash—'

He laughed, the sound bitter in his throat. 'You're honestly going to deny it? Then tell me, Zoey. Please. How am I different? What makes this any different from any of your other non-weddings?'

'Because I'm in love with you!'

The moment the words were out, Zoey wished she could take them back again—could rewind her life, all the way back to that night in the hotel, with another window she couldn't fit through. She'd have walked out of that cupboard and married David, if it meant she didn't have to see the look of horror on Ash's face at her words.

But they were out there now. So he might as well know everything. Maybe it would help him understand—forgive her even, one day.

Maybe he'd realise what a lucky escape they'd had, right here, today.

'I'm in love with you, and I know you can

never love me.' She sank back to lean against the bathroom counter, holding onto the Formica for added support. 'Grace was your true love; I get that. And I know you wanted the future you lost with her. But I can't do it, Ash.'

'Then why did you say yes when I proposed?' His voice was low with barely restrained anger. Zoey looked down at her bare toes to avoid seeing the hate in his eyes.

'Because…oh, because I wanted to be able to give you that. I wanted to be the one to give you your happily-ever-after. Your family, your future. Because I love you, and I wanted you to be happy.'

Was it her imagination, or did he actually flinch when she said the *L* word?

'So what changed?'

'I…' What was it? One big thing, or too many little things? Was it the way he kissed her goodnight and she always waited to hear him say *I love you*, and her heart broke a little more when it never came? Or was it her thinking of Grace in the car that morning? Or his father saying '*different from last time*'?

Or maybe it was all just the same, big thing.

Zoey swallowed, hard, and made herself say the words.

'I realised I can't spend the rest of my life trying to live up to a ghost, even one I loved as much as Grace. I love *you* too much, and knowing I'll never be enough for you would destroy me, in the end. So I'm sorry, but I can't marry you, Ash.'

And with that she picked up her shoes and, leaving them dangling from her fingers, walked out of the registry office, past Mr and Mrs Carmichael and a confused-looking registrar, and out into the street.

Time to start over. Again.

Ash stared after her as the bathroom door swung closed. Then, after a moment, he realised he was standing alone in the ladies' loos, and moved out into the corridor—only to find his parents and the registrar waiting for him.

'We heard shouting,' his mother said with an apologetic smile.

'The wedding's off,' Ash replied.

'Yes, we rather gathered that,' Arthur said, looking uncomfortable at the outpouring of emotion. Ash imagined he was wishing he was back behind his desk. 'And why, for that matter.'

His mother placed an arm around his shoulders, even though she had to reach up almost a foot to do it, even in heels. 'Come on, darling. Let's take you home—back to Kent with us. Everything will look a lot brighter in the morning, I'm sure.'

Ash let himself be ushered towards the door, his mind still reeling with Zoey's words.

She loved him. *Him*, Ash Carmichael.

She wasn't running because he wasn't enough for her—or, wait, maybe she was. Because he couldn't give her what she needed.

Because he wasn't in love with her.

Except…

'I have to say, son. A woman with a love and passion like that?' Arthur shook his head.

'I'm not sure I could let her just walk away.' Ash blinked. That might be the most personal thing his father had ever said to him.

And letting her walk away was what every other fiancé had done, wasn't it? They'd let Zoey walk out of their lives, and lived with the loss.

But he wasn't like all the others; she'd said so herself.

And now, faced with the prospect of a future without Zoey in it, he realised something else.

This wasn't about the baby. It wasn't about recreating the future he'd lost.

That wasn't why he'd asked Zoey to marry him. Or if it was at the start, it wasn't now.

Now, he wanted to marry her because of the way she brightened up his life—literally and figuratively. For the way his apartment was suddenly somewhere he wanted to be, now it was filled with her scent and her laugh and her everything in it. For the way she melted against him in bed at night, and he felt as if he'd come home at last. For the way her kiss made the world feel right. For how she made him laugh, or listened to him talk—and how he could listen to her for hours and never be bored.

Because she was his best friend.

And because he was in love with her too. Even if he'd been too much of an blind fool to realise it until now.

Grace would be rolling her eyes so hard right now, calling us both idiots.

And she'd be happy for them too, he was sure.

Because he knew now for certain what his happily-ever-after was—and what he hoped Zoey's was too.

He just had to find a way to make it happen.

Ash stopped suddenly in the doorway to the registry office. 'Dad? I'm going to need more than the week's leave I'd planned for the honeymoon. And there's something else I need that you can help me with too…'

CHAPTER FOURTEEN

SHE HAD NOWHERE to go. Again.

Zoey hailed a cab easily on the street, then sat in the back, uncertain of where to direct it.

'I do need an address, miss,' the cabbie said gently. Clearly he'd clocked the wedding dress and got an idea of how badly her day was going.

'Right. Yes. Um...' She gave Ash's address. All her stuff was still there, apart from anything else. Even if it did feel a bit like returning to the scene of the crime.

The door banged into the wall, the sound echoing around the flat as she walked in, alone. Her cheeks were wet, she realised as she brushed the tears away. She'd probably been crying ever since she'd left the registry office, and just not noticed.

She had a feeling there were a lot more tears to come.

Would Ash come back to the flat too? She thought not. He'd probably be whisked off by his parents for some TLC. And to give her a chance to get out of the flat. One of them would probably be here with an eviction notice before tomorrow.

Two suitcases leant against the wall by the door, packed and ready for the honeymoon they'd never take now. Ignoring them, Zoey moved through the flat like a ghost, drifting aimlessly down the hallway to the bedroom she'd not used since the night Ash had cooked her dinner and taken her to bed.

Her heart clenched as she passed the nursery, its sunny yellow too happy for her mood.

Her child would never sleep there now, probably. She had no idea where they *would* sleep, but she'd figure it out.

Because this wasn't like every other time she'd walked out on a wedding. This time, there were more consequences than moving out of a flat or giving back a ring.

She was still pregnant with Ash's baby, even if she hadn't married him. She couldn't just cut him out of her life the way she had all the others.

They had to find a way to move forward together, but apart. And that was a hell of a lot harder, she suspected.

But tomorrow. She'd figure it all out tomorrow.

Today, she just wanted to cry and sleep.

Reaching her bedroom, she flopped onto the bed face first and let the tears fall in earnest.

Tomorrow she'd be an adult again.

Today, her heart was too broken.

The sound of the door buzzer woke her, hours later, and she stumbled to it blearily.

'Hello?'

'Hello, Miss Hepburn. I'm here to take you to the airport. If you could just buzz me in, I'll come collect the bags.' It was the same driver from earlier, she realised, the one who'd taken her to the wedding. Ash must not have cancelled the transfer for their honeymoon, afterwards.

'Oh, no, there's no need. We're not going away after all.'

'Miss Hepburn, Mr Carmichael called me twenty minutes ago and asked me to collect you and your bags and take you to the airport. So if you could just buzz me in?'

Twenty minutes ago? Zoey leant against the buzzer as she checked her phone. One message.

Zoey, get in the car. We need to talk. A

Well. She had no idea what was going on, but Ash was right about one thing. They definitely needed to talk.

'Guess I'd better get changed then,' she said.

Apparently adulting started today, after all.

Ash paced the main open-plan living space of the villa, from the wide glass bifold doors that led out to the sea and back to the floor-to-ceiling windows on the other side, looking out over the beach. And then he did it again. And again.

When would she get there?

At least he knew she was coming; he'd had confirmation of take-off and, having made it all the way out to the Indian Ocean, he couldn't imagine her turning back again.

But she wasn't there yet. Hence the pacing.

He'd known that if they'd flown out there together, they'd have argued. As much as he wanted to fix things, Ash knew himself well enough to know he needed time to think his way through everything rationally—and Zoey probably did too. So he'd taken a commercial flight out, and asked his father to arrange the charter for Zoey and their bags.

Which meant now he had to wait.

The villa was almost unrecognisable from the place they'd stayed that fateful night. The renovations had been completed at last, and the whole place was the pinnacle of the luxury travel experience Carmichael's sought to provide. From the designer seating to the carefully selected palette of colours, everything screamed expensive—and, more importantly, the best.

Ash just hoped Zoey would understand what he was trying to do by bringing her here.

He wanted to start again. To give them a fresh chance to get this right. Whatever *this* turned out to be.

Ash knew what he wanted, what dreams kept him awake at night. But he also knew that the decision had to be Zoey's. If she wanted to run still, he wouldn't try to keep her.

But if there was a chance she really could want the same life together that he did…well, he had to take it.

As his pacing reached the glass doors again, he saw something in the distance, kicking up spray from the waves. A small motor boat, racing closer through the surf.

And there, right at the front, looking out towards him, was Zoey—her hair streaming back from her face, her sundress blown tight against her by the air current.

Ash opened the doors and headed out onto

the jetty to greet her, his eyes greedily drinking in every sight of her, even as the boat bobbed closer.

Was that a small bump, shown off by the thin fabric of her sundress? He thought it might be, and the realisation filled him with a warmth and excitement he barely recognised.

He was going to be a father. Whatever else happened between them, whatever the future held, that much was still true.

And yes, he was terrified of it being torn away from him again—and, given Zoey's history, he'd be an idiot not to acknowledge the flight risk.

But she'd said *'I love you'* and he believed her.

Which was why he had to give this his best shot.

The motor boat slowed and docked alongside the jetty, the driver hopping out to tie it up securely. Ash stepped forward and offered Zoey his hand to help her off the boat. She looked at him for a moment before taking it, and he wished more than anything that he could read her mind right then.

'You came,' he said.

She gave him a funny half smile. 'Seemed rude not to, really. Besides, I have a new rule. I came up with it on the plane. No more running away from things, however scary they are.'

Something tightened in Ash's chest. 'Good. Because I think we have a lot to talk about.'

It felt so strange, sitting inside such a high-end luxury villa—which was somehow also the shell of a building they'd spent the night in together.

'How was your journey?' Ash asked as he fussed around her—taking her bags, fetching her a drink of juice, finding more cushions for the sofa.

'Let's just say that it's a good job the morning sickness really did finally pass at twelve weeks.' She shuddered, trying to imagine that flight with the constant nausea that had accompanied her through the pregnancy so far.

Ash froze, halfway through plumping a pillow. 'I didn't even think about that. I should have done. I shouldn't have asked you to fly all this way when you're pregnant. I just—'

'Ash.' She placed a hand over his and pulled him to sit down next to her on the sofa. 'I know why you wanted me to come out here.'

'You do?' He sounded surprised.

Zoey smiled. 'Of course I do.' She'd had a lengthy flight alone to think about it, on one of the Carmichael's private planes. 'It's where it all started for us. And if we want to move forward as parents and friends, we have to go back and fix everything we got wrong between here and there.'

She should have known that Ash wouldn't give up their friendship, just because she was an idiot. And it wasn't as if he'd been in love with her anyway, so leaving him at the altar wouldn't have broken his heart or anything.

They could fix this. They might never be together again, and that hurt. But at least she knew they'd make things right for their child.

'Yeah, I guess that's pretty much it,' Ash admitted. 'So, where do we start?'

Zoey took a deep breath. She'd practised what she wanted to say on the plane, over and over. But saying it to his face, when he was watching her so carefully, felt like a whole different challenge.

'With an apology. And an explanation.'

'I think you said everything you needed to at the registry office,' Ash said. 'Well, apart from the apology.'

'I'm sorry,' Zoey said automatically. 'I should have talked to you, not run.'

'You should. But I'm sorry too.'

'What for? I was the one who tried to escape through a window. Again.'

'But I was the one who railroaded you into marriage. I should have known better.' Ash shook his head. 'I knew you were still looking for your true love, your happy ending. And as far as you were concerned I was asking you to give up all that to marry me.'

'I guess,' Zoey said, a large lump forming in her throat. She forced the words out around it. 'You're right—all I've ever wanted was a loving, happy marriage and maybe a family, one day. I wanted to do it all right—the way my parents didn't. I wanted what you and Grace had—and you already told me you couldn't give me that.'

'I did say that,' Ash admitted. 'Because I am an idiot.'

'I couldn't steal the future Grace was meant to have and lost,' Zoey went on, ignoring him. Then his words caught up with her. 'What?'

Ash moved across from her so his gaze could meet hers. He stared deep into her eyes, as if he was searching for the truth behind her words. Zoey made herself hold his gaze and let him look.

After all, her truths were already lying between them.

'Did you mean what you said? At the registry office?' he asked.

'Which part?'

'The part where you're in love with me?'

Zoey looked away. 'A bit. Sorry.'

Ash laughed, a low, husky chuckle. 'Love, don't be sorry. Hearing those words from you woke me up.'

Zoey blinked. 'What?'

'You made me realise how much I'd given up on. I'd tried to move forward, replacing what I'd lost—but I hadn't ever opened myself up fully to the future. I hadn't given myself the chance of finding something *new*. A different future for me—and for you.'

'I don't understand.'

'Then I realised that all your previous fiancés had something in common,' Ash went on, adding to her confusion.

'Yes. I ran out on them. Every time,' Zoey pointed out.

'With good reason.' Ash shuddered. 'I am *so* glad you didn't marry any of them. Not least because it would make it much harder for you to marry me.'

'I thought we agreed we weren't doing that?'

'I'm hoping what I'm about to say will change your mind,' Ash replied.

'You're talking about my ex-boyfriends,'

Zoey said. 'I'm not really sure this is going to work.'

'Give me a chance.' Ash smiled—an honest, open, *happy* smile—and Zoey tried to remember the last time she'd seen that. When she was naked, probably.

'Okay.' Was that hope, tingling low in her belly?

'The point was, I realised that they all let you go. None of them followed you, tried to find out what you wanted and give it to you. So that's what I want to do now.'

The hope died. 'Ash, I told you what I need from a marriage and you can't give it to me.'

'You want love,' Ash replied. 'And the thing is… I always knew I loved you—you were Zoey, part of my family, of course I loved you.'

'Like a friend. Or a sister,' Zoey said glumly. 'That's not what I mean.'

'Yes. Except…not at all. Not even a little bit, it turns out.' Ash grabbed her hands and made her look at him again, and she saw something burning, deep in his eyes. Something she'd never even let herself look for before, or hope for.

'Ash?' she asked softly. She needed to hear the words.

'When you walked out on me, I realised I was so in love with you I couldn't think straight.'

It felt so good to have said it. To have the knowledge out there in the world, not stuck inside his head. And the warm glow of cautious happiness that Zoey was emitting at hearing it made every bit of the last couple of days worthwhile.

'I spent so long looking back at what I'd lost, I think I forgot how to look forward,' he whispered. 'But you showed me how again. And when you left I knew that I had to let go of the past and build a new future. I hope, with you.'

Reaching out, Ash pulled Zoey towards him, tracing a hand across her cheek to the back of her neck as he kissed her—gently but deeply, and hopefully full of all the words he still had to say to her.

She kissed him back, warm and loving, and Ash was filled with a sense of incredible good fortune. How could he be so lucky as to have found love like this not once, but twice?

A small part of him even wondered if this could be Grace's doing, matchmaking from the afterlife. He wouldn't put it past her. She always wanted her loved ones to be happy, more than anything.

Eventually, they broke the kiss. Ash rested his forehead against Zoey's and smiled down at her.

'So. Do you think I stand a better chance of convincing you to marry me now?' he asked.

Suddenly, Zoey's happy glow faded and she pulled away. 'Ash...'

'No.' He grabbed her hand and held it tight. 'No running, remember?'

She gave him a weak smile. 'I'm not sure I could if I wanted to. Give me another couple of months and I'll be hard pressed to even *waddle* away from you.'

And he couldn't wait to see it. To see her, heavy and blooming with his child. To know that they would be a *family,* just like they'd both always wanted.

But first he needed to figure out what the rest of her reservations were, and fix them. Quickly.

'You're beautiful,' he told her. 'Even green and vomiting, and definitely when you're nine months pregnant with my child. I promise you, I won't be able to get enough of you, even then.'

She gave him a disbelieving look. Maybe the bit about the vomit had been a little over the top.

'Zoey, tell me. What's the matter?'

Her teeth sank into her bottom lip as she chewed it, obviously weighing up her words. Her gaze didn't leave his, though, which he loved. He might not be able to read her thoughts, but he could see her emotions, passing behind her eyes.

She was still scared. He hated that she was scared of a future with him.

Ash knew better than anyone that the future could be a terrifying and unpredictable place. But he couldn't let that stop him hoping for better. He knew that now.

He hoped she did.

'I can't shake the feeling that I'm stealing Grace's place,' she admitted. 'Or that you're going to wake up one day next to me, and realise you're still wishing I was someone else. That I'll never be enough to replace her.'

'You're not replacing her. You couldn't.' He said it softly, but he saw the way his words made her flinch, all the same. 'Zo, do you think I haven't been thinking about Grace too? I do, every day. And I'm not going to stop—the same way you won't. But she's gone. She's been gone a long time now, and I know that we can't live our lives in a limbo, waiting in case of a miracle that won't come.'

'I know that too,' Zoey muttered, but she wasn't looking at him again now.

Ash tucked a finger under her chin and nudged her head up so she had to meet his eyes.

'Here's what I've realised,' he said. 'Grace will always be my first love. But that doesn't make my love for you any less. I love you, Zoey.'

Were those tears in her eyes? He hated to make her cry, but he needed to say this. And he had a feeling she needed to hear it.

'I'm not the same man I was when I married Grace. I'm not even the same man I was when she died. Two years of grief change a man. But, more than that, *you* changed me. Not just in one night here on this island, or even the months since. Before all of that, your love and care and kindness changed me. Every time you picked me up off the floor from a drunken, grief-filled stupor. Every time you sat all night with me and shared memories of Grace. Every time you called to check in, or texted a joke to make me laugh. *You* changed me, Zoey. Until I knew that if something happened in my life, you were the person I wanted to tell. Until you were the person I wanted to see last thing at night and first thing in the morning. Until you were the person whose opinion mattered, whose feelings counted most, who I'd drop everything and sail into a storm for.

'I might not have known that I loved you before this week. But, looking back, I can see my love for you—and yours for me—stretching back. The type of love it is changed that night on this island, when we realised how much we *wanted* each other too. But that wasn't where it started. That's only the latest part of it.'

'And now we have a whole new love story to tell.' Zoey placed his hand against her belly, where his child grew, and Ash thought his heart might explode from the rightness of it all.

'Yours might not have been the love I chose first, Zoey, but I promise you it'll be the last love I ever need. And I'll keep choosing you, and our family, day after day, for the rest of my life. If you'll let me.'

He could see her blinking away tears as she replied, 'Of course I will. You're my happily-ever-after.'

Ash smiled. 'I hope so. But, right now, our story is only just beginning.'

EPILOGUE

THE BEACH WAS packed with friends and family. At least she wasn't naked on it this time. Zoey winced, sparing a thought for the poor guys who'd rescued them off this very same island eighteen months ago, after the storm, when she'd waved her dress over her head as she ran towards them naked. Ash didn't seem to think they'd minded all that much, though.

When she'd asked Ash why he'd insisted on buying the villa—and the island—back from the company for his own personal use, he'd told her it was *their* place. Where it had all started, for real. And he couldn't imagine sharing it with anyone else.

But they were, this weekend at least. Of course, after the ceremony and the reception, Ash had laid on boats to take everyone away again to neighbouring island hotels, so they could spend their wedding night in peace, in their place.

Ash had flown all their guests out on the company plane, and somehow nobody had objected to attending yet another of her weddings, this time. Zoey imagined it was because of what they could see when they looked at Ash and her together, especially with little baby Charlie there with them too.

It was the same thing Zoey felt every time the three of them were together—which was as much of the time as possible.

Happiness.

True, happily-ever-after happiness.

It felt funny to think that after all those years chasing the perfect future, the ideal husband, she'd almost run away from the real thing when she'd found him.

Zoey smiled to herself. Maybe the reason it had all worked out was that Ash was the first one to actually chase *her*.

'So. Still want to do this?' Ash came up behind her, wrapping his arms around the waist of her bright pink wedding dress and holding her close.

'Where's Charlie?' she asked.

'Playing with his grandpa. He's having a great time,' Ash assured her. 'And I told Dad not to let him eat any more sand, so we're probably fine.'

Zoey wasn't entirely sure how thrilled Arthur would be about playing babysitter instead of enjoying the free bar, but it was true that Charlie adored his grandpa—and his grandpa loved him too. Maybe even more than Carmichael Luxury Travel, much to everyone's amazement.

'I ask you again. Are you sure you want to go through with it this time? Marrying me, I mean.'

Zoey twisted around in his arms and smiled up at him. 'Is that why you wanted us to stay here together last night? In case I decided to run again?'

Ash shook his head. 'No. I wanted to stay here with you because I can't bear to be apart from you. And if you want to run, I'd run with you, if you'd let me.'

'And if I wouldn't?'

'Then I'd let you go. Reluctantly, because it would break my heart. But seriously, Zo.' He looked down at her, all laughter gone from his eyes. 'If you need to run, just tell me.'

Oh, but she loved him. So much.

'Ash, you and Charlie, you're my home. My future.' She placed a hand against his cheek. 'Where on earth could I run to without leaving my heart behind? There is nowhere in the world I would rather be right now than here with you. Besides, I told you. No more running. Ever.'

'So we're getting married?' Ash asked.

She pressed a kiss to his lips. 'We're getting married.'

'Thank heavens for that.' Ash's gaze shifted away from hers and over her shoulder. 'Um, that no running thing, though. Does it still count if Charlie's eating sand again?'

Zoey glanced back at where her son was sitting at Arthur's feet, feeding himself sand as Arthur chatted to one of his many business contacts.

'Come on.' She grabbed Ash's hand and together they ran across the sand towards their son, the altar, and their happily-ever-after.

* * * * *

LET'S TALK

For exclusive extracts, competitions and special offers, find us online:

 f facebook.com/millsandboon

 ⭕ @millsandboonuk

 🐦 @millsandboon

Or get in touch on 0844 844 1351*

For all the latest titles coming soon, visit millsandboon.co.uk/nextmonth

*Calls cost 7p per minute plus your phone company's price per minute access charge